IRONCLADS

ADRIAN TCHAIKOVSKY

SOLARIS

First published 2017 by Solaris
an imprint of Rebellion Publishing Ltd,
Riverside House, Osney Mead,
Oxford, OX2 0ES, UK

www.solarisbooks.com

ISBN: 978-1-78108-568-4

10 9 8 7 6 5 4 3 2 1

A CIP catalogue record for this book is available from
the British Library.

Designed & typeset by Rebellion Publishing

Printed and bound by CPI Group (UK) Ltd, Croydon, CR0 4YY

ONE OF 1000 LIMITED EDITION COPIES

GREENWICH LIBRARIES

3 8028 02347322 3

IRONCLADS

With thanks to my special military advisers
Harry Cattes, Shane McLean and Rick Wynne

CHAPTER ONE

STURGEON SAYS THAT, way back when, the sons of the rich used to go to war as a first choice of career. He says that, back then, the regular grunts were basically just poor bastards with a knife and a leather jacket – only he's got that annoying-as-crap patronising look that says he's dumbing stuff down for me – and no training, and no clue, save what lies they got told.

But the rich guys: Sturgeon says they had all the time in the world to learn stuff, and all the money in the world, and they bought the best armor that no poor bastard was going to stick a knife through, and they would just wade in and make a game of how many poor bastards they could cut up on the way. And even if things went really bad for them, they didn't die, Sturgeon says. He says they just let themselves get captured and ransomed, and had a fine old time telling jokes to the rich guys who grabbed them about all the poor bastards they killed.

What Sturgeon says is that things swung round – the science of killing a man sort of galloped ahead of the science of stopping him being killed. Guns, mostly. And suddenly the sons of the rich didn't like the idea of being soldiers, not once it was them getting shot up with the rest of the poor bastards. The clever ones went to war with a crapton of gold braid on their sleeves and a crapton of space between them and the front lines. The rest went into stock-brokering and lawyering and running companies, where the money was better and the chance of getting shot was less, and you still basically got to say how the war went, if you were in the right industry.

But they missed it, when it was gone, Sturgeon says. There's something you get from shooting a guy, from ripping his head off, from just wading in and showing the poor bastards how much better you are than them in the most simple, physical way. He reckons it's a kick you just don't get with raiding the company pension pot or evicting tenants or throwing a prostitute out of a window and getting away with it cos your uncle's a police chief and your grandfather's a judge.

Sturgeon says things have gone full circle. Sturgeon says a lot of stuff, though. Usually he doesn't get this far into his spiel before Franken slugs him. Sturgeon, as far as I'm concerned, is full of shit.

*　　*　　*

WE TOUCHED DOWN in England February 9th with about two thousand other tough guys out of the 203rd to rapturous applause. 'Rapturous applause' is Sturgeon again, but he was right: the limeys loved us. Mostly, they loved the fact we had money, which wasn't something the old country had much of. Everyone knew that a GI on shore leave anywhere in the English Territories had struck lucky. Women and booze were dirt cheap there, and if you got into a scrap and broke a window or an arm then the cops knew to look the other way. But that didn't happen often, or not on my watch. Weird thing how fond most of the guys were about England. Now it was part of the Union everyone was all 'the old country' and feeling mighty protective of the place, like all our ancestors had come over on the *Mayflower*.

My ancestors had come over from the greenish island next door, far as I know, and I reckoned I was let off feeling sentimental about the English on that count. Still, it was going to be a solid two weeks R&R before the 203rd got shipped off again to take the war to the Nords.

We got dumped off at the big base near Reading, leave shifts downloaded to our hub and the first mob of us already fixing to hit London and stuff some good solid dollars down some kinky dancers' panties. For the rest, it looked like half of England had come to us. There was a regular shanty town outside the base – they had a whole load of girls come here because it meant they could earn some cash to send home, and a bunch of older folks who had sad little stalls and carts and tents, selling everything from beer to little tin statues of Big Ben, from the wisdom of the druids to the family silver. They looked… they looked thin and dirty and tired. That was what England looked like to me. Thin and dirty and tired, and with those bad teeth you hear about – that Sturgeon says was never a thing back then, but sure as hell is now. And smoking. Everyone smoked there, the cheapest, nastiest cigarettes you ever ended up stinking of. Which they called fags, which was good for a laugh at least.

Sturgeon has a bundle to say about that, as well. Of course he does, the mouthy bastard. Sturgeon says that it wasn't much more than twenty years after they voted in their Independence crowd and cut themselves right off from Europe, before those same politicos sold the whole shebang to us. Turned out England couldn't stand on its little Union Jack-gartered legs the way it once had, but that was fine: its new leaders had already got themselves a place on the board at a dozen US corporations, so they were all right. Anyway, England became a territory of the Union, and the media said everyone was happy about that.

Later, it became our stepping stone for taking the good fight into Europe, when it turned out that we had what Sturgeon calls irreconcilable ideological differences with some of the governments there.

The base was busy – they already had the 12th Mountaineers and some armor there, and a whole load of the 170th were just being flown out. We were all getting billeted – and more than ready to get down to other things too, the moment we had the chance – when I remember Franken punching me in the shoulder, which is how he gets your attention.

"Sarge, lookit," says Franken.

I lookited, and I saw what he was talking about, and it's a hell of a sight: no fewer than three Scions striding through the press of the base like it was nothing, and everyone else getting the hell out of their way.

The English call them 'the Brass,' but to us they're just Scions. This is who Sturgeon was bitching about, with his dumb history lesson. I squinted at them as they strode past, looking for the logos; looked like a pair from the pharma giant Sayline and one – the biggest one – from the agricorp Buenosol, who are pushing so much of the action over in Nordland. They were eight feet tall, give or take, and you couldn't have gotten the edge of a razor anywhere into the joints of their armored shells. One of the Sayline boys was like an egg on spider legs but the other two were built like men, two arms, two legs on a big armored box where the actual lucky guy would be sitting with all home comforts. They had more guns each than a whole squad, and there was nothing the 203rd was equipped with that would have got through that plating of theirs, either. It felt like a privilege to be this close to them and everyone had gone quiet when they came through. Some, like Franken, pushed close to get a touch, a hand on that expensive metal, because if you were into that stuff the Church of Christ Libertarian went on about, these guys were the Deserving. These guys were rich because it was God's plan, just like if any of us got rich, that would be God's plan too. Just like any one of us might get rich, somehow. We could be the president too. Everyone said so. We just had to work hard and wait our turn.

Anyway, the three Scions just shoved their way through

us all, not giving us a glance, and Franken was practically drooling, no doubt imagining how it would be to fight a war from inside a metal shell like that, with a comfy seat and porn on demand and a machine to wipe your ass for you. And I heard Sturgeon do one of those 'tsk' noises he does, because, like I've probably made clear, Sturgeon's an asshole with Ideas and Opinions, and neither of those things is much use for an infantryman these days.

Ninety minutes after touching down at Reading, me, Sturgeon and Franken got our orders to get on a heli for London, and none of us had the faintest idea why. My best guess was that Sturgeon's mouth had got him into trouble, and that Franken and I had been luckless enough to be within earshot. Nobody told us what was going on, we just got passed hand to hand, airport to car, car to city center, along the Embankment road with those bigass barriers to stop the river coming in all their posh lobbies, and then we ended up at the top of a glass-steel tower in whatever they called Wall Street over in London, waiting in a boardroom where the chairs probably cost more than any of us would earn in ten years.

Franken was looking knives at Sturgeon. To be honest, so was I. Sturgeon was a tall, narrow-shouldered New Yorker with a nose like an elbow, and when he wasn't about you'd have said he had glasses on – even though nobody in the army wore glasses – just because he was like so many speccy nerd guys in old TV shows. He wasn't a computer geek or a business wiz or any of those useful sorts of nerds, though, or he wouldn't have been slogging about with a gun like the rest of us. Sturgeon was just a guy who'd had way too much education and then found he had way too little money, like all of us had way too little money. These days the army was often the best, sometimes the only, way of digging yourself out of that hole.

Franken was blonde and from Kentucky and the size of three Sturgeons mashed together, which was a fact he'd had cause to impress on Sturgeon more than once in the time I'd known them. I'd been with them both in Uruguay and then in Canada, and I'd always reckoned that we'd end up going our separate ways after one tour or another. And yet, whenever I got back off leave, it was their ugly faces I was showing the family photos to. The three of us had been on 203rd HQ's Recon platoon through more clusterfucks than I cared to remember.

Sturgeon opened his mouth and I could see he was going to say something clever, meaning something that would get us into trouble. "They're listening," I told his open mouth, and he shut it quickly. No sense getting us into worse than we already were.

"What, then?" Franken demanded.

"We might not even be in the shit," I remember saying, without much enthusiasm. "Maybe they just need security or something. Maybe this is it: easy street for the rest of the war."

"Us?" Franken pointed out. "The three of us get a soft security detail? Because, stop me if I'm wrong, don't they have their own people for that? You know, the real corporate guys, rather than army?"

"Yeah, well," I started, and then the Man came in.

I called them to attention, but I didn't have to, we were already on the way there: me, Franken, Sturgeon, one after the other. You always stand to attention when a Scion's there. A Scion always outranks a regular soldier.

He was seven foot tall and must have weighed six hundred pounds in his suit; not all the lightweight alloys in the world could bring that down. These days, every boardroom in the west had reinforced floors and extra-wide doors. His suit shone like it had just been polished. There was a head on top – it wouldn't have had the guy's head in it, it was just for show – that was square-jawed and good-looking as a film star, and the whole chassis was moulded like the muscles of a weightlifter. I'd run into a few Scions by then, and his was by far the nicest piece of kit I'd seen: fancy enough that I reckoned it was his peacetime civvies, and that he probably had a spikier suit for wartime. A lot of the Scions didn't get out of their shells unless they were inside their compounds, behind a dozen walls and a hundred guards. After all, there was still the occasional bomber out there, home-grown or foreign national. Sons and nephews of the corporate board members were too valuable to take risks with, even here in London City Central.

On his shoulder, like I had my stripes, there was a little logo, but I didn't know it. Scions from companies you hadn't heard of were Big Business. If a company was too small for you to have heard of it, it couldn't afford Scion shells for its gallant warrior sons. If a Scion came from somewhere that wasn't a household name, that meant it was one of the big, hidden companies; the companies that owned the companies that you knew.

When he spoke, a face came up over the cold steel of the mask. Probably it was his face; what would have been the point else? It was a good looking, well-groomed regular guy sort of face, just like they all had when they were rich enough. It wasn't the sort of face anyone was born with, but one that had been measured and tweaked and shaved until it said: *I Am Right; and You Can Trust Me.* You liked that face, just looking at it; you trusted it; you wanted it to like you.

"At ease, Gentlemen. Thanks for coming," said the projected face. His voice was just as well crafted, elocuted and touched up. You'd have done a lot, if that voice asked you. "You would be Theodore Regan, I take it?"

"Yes sir, Sergeant Ted Regan, sir."

He smiled at me, one of those magic smiles where all the condescension is invisible. "I'm a Ted too. Ted Speling, looking after the family interests over here while the war's on." He didn't offer to shake hands. With Scions, it was a habit that had fallen out of use. "Sergeant Regan, you're in a position to do my family a favor."

He said that, and I already wanted to help him any way I could. Plus, of course, that sounded like there was money in it. And then he said: "My cousin Jerome has gone missing, Sergeant. Something happened to him three days ago, out on the front. Nobody knows where he is. You men come highly recommended. I need you to find him, or find what happened to him. Will you do that for me?"

Of course I would. I was already agreeing to it. I didn't choke over that 'highly recommended' bit (because, *really? Us?*). I didn't even see the Big Thing in what he'd said until Sturgeon finally burned through his ability to keep his mouth shut and said, "Your cousin was on the front, sir?"

"That's correct, soldier," said Rich Ted.

Even as I – Poor Ted – was shooting a glare at him, Sturgeon's mouth went right on motoring. "Was he out of his shell, sir?"

And I stopped, because he was right: any cousin Jerome that Ted Speling might lay claim to wouldn't have been within a hundred miles of the front without a shell.

"Well," Rich Ted said philosophically. "It so happens you've hit on the very heart of the problem."

Even then I thought that Cousin Jerome must have decided to get out of his shell, take the breeze or something; maybe there was some pretty little Nord girl tricked him into it. It's pretty much the only need that those suits only fulfil halfway, after all. But no; Cousin Jerome hadn't been pressing his *dwat de sey-nyer*, as Sturgeon called it. The enemy had done something, and his shell had just cut out and shut down and stopped telling anyone where it was.

You see, that never happened. There was a lot of tech in the world, and while we poor grunts got just enough to do our jobs, the Scions got everything money could buy. They had all the money, after all. Sturgeon says – here I go again with what Sturgeon says, but – he says that back when soldiers were soldiers, there was a whole lot of money put into making sure we had all we needed to let us return in one piece – it was lost votes and bad PR if all your brave boys didn't make it back to the Land of the Free. Of course we've had the means-tested voting reforms since then – what the newspapers when I was a kid called the 'Elephant in the Room', on account of how so many people had just become something nobody talked about. Now, on account of regular soldiering being a good job for people with no other options, Sturgeon says, when we get cut up, it doesn't impact on the election so much. This is when he starts saying how the government doesn't look after us any more, and this is usually where Franken starts hitting him.

But sure, it's no secret that your regular grunt does not get the dollars spent on him that the corporate squads do, in terms of gear and support, and it's true we get the crap jobs that they don't, because if things do get hot for us, it's the government footing the bill, not the corporations. And I might have some thoughts and feelings about that, but because I'm not so damn smart as Sturgeon, I keep my mouth shut.

And Scions – Scions have no limits, or certainly the models made in the US of A don't. Those shells are the battledress of the sons of corporations. No man of means is going to send his heir or his spare out with anything less than the best – just like they wouldn't be seen dead in anything less than the biggest car, or perfect teeth, or what golf club you belonged to. When I was in Canada, I saw... well, when our shining boys came through, you should have seen the Canuck infantry run like rabbits. And when their maple-leaf ironclads came stomping the other way, we couldn't hold, even though everyone said they weren't as good. We couldn't dent them.

Sturgeon says that we could have done, only they didn't give us the tools for it. He says that all the corporate types go to the same clubs, and that it's not in their interests to kill each other off when there might be a merger the week after. Like I say, Sturgeon says a lot of things.

Nonetheless, this is beyond dispute: better than the regulars, better than the best-equipped corporate guard, better than mechs and drones and biotech is the armor and the weaponry of the battlefield Scions.

Which brings us back to Cousin Jerome, because all that top flight tech had just fucked off and deserted him, and now he was either dead or caught. Rich Ted was pretty sure he was caught; Jerome would be a big old bargaining chip for the Nords, after all, except that apparently nobody was even asking for a ransom.

That made it our job to go get him. Or to find his body or records of his demise. At no point did he say anything about finding out how the hell they screwed over his shell to winkle him out of it, but that was kind of hanging in the air in a 'bonus payment' sort of way. I reckon they wouldn't honestly have trusted us with that one as a mission objective, but if it fell into our laps we surely would be bringing it to Rich Ted's rich attention.

"Why us, sir?" I asked, and he explained that we would be going in as a small, covert team. He talked about the fact that we three had come through some of the nastier global knife-fights of the last few years without a scratch, and with commendations – he didn't mention all those times Sturgeon got put on a charge for opening his big, big mouth, or when Franken almost got court martialed for punching a captain. He said a lot of things, but I was used to Sturgeon, and so I could cut through the crap. "You want this done, why not send a few unstoppable Scions?" I could have asked, and the answer he would never have given me was: "Because we're scared they'll do it to us."

Two hours later we were on a plane heading seaward toward the fighting, detached from 203rd's Recon company and leaving the rest of the lads behind. You'd think one of the officers might have made a fuss, but everyone knew that when the Corporates said "jump," you basically didn't come down without orders in triplicate. We were there to fight the war their way, and if their way was sending the three of us off on a rescue mission then that was what was going to happen.

There was gear for us in the plane – and it was brand new, not the hand-me-down crap we normally had to work with. Franken complained, of course. Franken liked his own stuff, worn by long use until it was a comfortable fit in his big hands and smelling mostly of Franken. For me, I appreciated the downpayment. This was Rich Ted investing in Poor Ted, at least a little.

We slept on the plane; live this life long enough and you sleep when you can. The plane's descent woke us and when we looked out, we saw Nord country.

CHAPTER TWO

STURGEON SAID, ONE time, about how the barriers broke in New York when he was a kid and suddenly the whole city was fighting a desperate rearguard action against the sea; when the Hudson burst its banks and swallowed Bloomfield and half of Newark, and made an island out of Newark Liberty Airport. It was the same on both coasts, the defining images of the decade as all that denial came home to roost. But not for Nordland, apparently. Sturgeon said that it was geology, basically; that all this mountainous, fjord-cut land was still riding high even as the sea clawed at it, keeping just ahead of the tide while Thailand and New Orleans and the Netherlands went the way of Atlantis.

The beachhead was a place called Gotham-berg – or that's what everyone called it. The place was thoroughly home-away-from-home. We came in to a chorus of accents from Texas and New England and everywhere in between, and the first thing that met our eyes when we got off the plane was a Mickey-D's. The fighting was way north and east of there. Gotham was thoroughly pacified and brought round to our way of thinking. Of the rest of the country...

Sturgeon got really obsessive about it, when we talked about fighting the Nords. Then he got hit, mostly, but basically there are a lot of Nords, and we're not fighting all of them. The bit just over the sea west of Gotham hasn't weighed in yet, and there's another lot up in a long strip on the west coast who are apparently still mulling it over, with a buttload of Marines waiting just offshore in case they come to the wrong decision any time soon. All the middle of Nordland is the bit we've got problems with, basically: Sweden and Finland, say the maps. Sweden is where the fighting is, and the other place... Finland is weird. Finland is different. Nobody I met in Nordland was looking forward to when Sweden had given it over, and we were left looking at the Finnish border and all the ungodly shit that was waiting on the other side.

We got orders pretty much as soon as we hit tarmac: we had to meet the rest of our team. What rest of our team, you might ask? Apparently Rich Ted didn't want to rely on us quite that much, so we cooled our heels in the vast expanse of Gotham that had been given over as a staging post, waiting for the pair of them to pitch up. We got to watch our boys and the armor and the gleaming god-statues of the Scions march off to stick it to the Nords, and we got to watch a fair number of our boys come back bloodied, though we reckoned we were giving far more than we got.

What it was – this is Sturgeon again – after all the levees broke, after the big economic crunch that hit when half our coastal cities turned into swimming pools, everyone needed to pull together. Pulling together, here, meant buying American, supporting the big corporations that were our only hope of rebuilding. The problem was that, over the pond, there were a whole load of governments who'd taken the same knocks and gone the other way, taken their god-given democracy and abused it to vote in the socialists. A whole bunch chucked out all those promises they made under the Transatlantic Free Trade Agreement. Corporate assets were seized. There were bombs, too – full-on terrorist attacks on the property of multinationals. They were fixing to take all that good stuff our corps had built up and grab it for themselves, just hand it over free to every Bjorn and Benny. It was, everyone says, an assault on our freedoms, on our very way of life. Everyone except Sturgeon, anyway, and I guess probably the Nords.

We kicked our heels for two days, which was fine – if there was anyone who knew how to have a good time on a US military base it was us poor bastards. Then Lawes and Cormoran turned up, and we were a team and ready to go.

Lawes and Cormoran had obviously been given the chance to get to know each other before they reached us, and there was a distance between them that told me neither of them had much enjoyed it. Lawes was a little guy, smaller than Sturgeon even, and there was nothing neat about him. I never saw him clean-shaved and his uniform was darned and filthy, dotted with old stains he hadn't been able to get out, and his shoes scuffed. He had brown teeth, huge in his thin face, like he'd been designed to gnaw through cables we'd find we needed later. He was a corporal in the English expeditionary force that got sent over when our boys first landed; he'd been here since the start, which made him our best shot at local knowledge. When I saw his gear, there was some serious snake-eater covert ops stuff there – gear that would make him room temperature to thermals and screw with motion sensors. He was someone who knew all the holes and the gaps in the fences; there was more than a touch of the rodent about Corporal Lawes.

Cormoran was a different beast altogether: some kind of predator, a panther maybe. She came with a metal suitcase that looked like it weighed a ton, and she had a lean, lanky body that could lug it around like it didn't weigh anything. Her fatigues were grey and expensive, and there was a shimmer about them that said they could do all sorts of things, just like her headset and the gadgets in that case. Cormoran was a woman, and black, but the truth was that Cormoran was corporate, and that set her apart from the rest of us far more. She got paid more, and she got better gear, and most of all she would surely have some personal mission to fulfil, or why would she even be here? I reckoned that going on a mission with Cormoran would be like travelling with a time bomb. We'd always be waiting for her to suddenly decide her objectives were more important than ours.

Not that we had a choice about taking her. We'd need her anyway: she was a drone specialist. Whilst mostly that should have meant she got to fight the war from a hundred miles behind the lines, these days the Nords had some good electronic countermeasures, which meant that a lot of fancy drone work was best done from inside the range of a gun. Lucky Cormoran; lucky all of us.

They shipped us out to the front. The 96th Armored and its friends were pushing east just then, taking ground from a Nord army which was mostly just backpedalling and letting them have it. Convoys would get us as far as the troops got, and after that we'd be on our own as we broke the line and headed into enemy territory. All we'd need to do would be to keep our heads down and stay clear of anything that had a Swedish flag while we closed in on Cousin Jerome's last known position.

"Except," Lawes told us on the way out, "it ain't as simple as that, is it? I mean sure, Swedish national army, easy enough. There ain't exactly that many of them, and the way I hear, your lot've got 'em on the back foot anyhow – if it was just them. But this bloody country – who'd've thought they'd got so much fight in 'em, eh?" He spat, smoked, twisting together horrible roll-ups with stringy tobacco from a yellow tin. "Stockholm's lost control, is the problem. There's Nord corporations fighting on both bloody sides – I got shelled by the 1st fighting corps of fucking Ikea last year! – and there's all sorts of wankers coming in from mainland Europe to fight for the Swedes – men and mechs and White Walkers. And the *locals*. Wherever you end up there are partisans, just civvies who've grabbed up whatever gear they can. And when the Nord army gets its orders to pull back, you think the partisans go with them? Don't you believe it. Every fjord and stream and hill and rock'll have some Sven or Olga with a gun. And then there are the Finns, always the bastard Finns."

"I heard about them," I told him.

Lawes fixed me with his rodent stare. "You ain't heard nothing. They ain't human any more, what they send over the border."

After that he tried to interest people in a card game, and Franken took him up on it and lost a few dollars – meant less to him than the win did to Lawes, but that's the English economy for you.

I tried to get Cormoran talking, picking a question just too flat-out rude to be ignored. "So how come someone like you lands a job like that?"

She gave me a look that said it wasn't the first time she'd heard that. "Summa cum laude out of MIT," and then, because she saw something in my face, "Yeah, before they changed admissions policy. Last class of Alpha Kappa Alpha, me." I didn't know what she meant, but I looked it up later.

I tried to push a little more, but she was having none of it, her dark, bony face closed off. There was something I saw there – the look of a woman who doesn't think it's worth getting to know you, in the short time you've got.

After that it got interesting. I was woken up when something exploded outside the plane and for a moment I didn't know where I was or which war I was fighting, just crunched and taut and bracing myself against everything, because it was all dipping and diving around me. Franken was swearing, but that didn't narrow it down because we'd been serving together a while and that was kind of his baseline.

Cormoran was the center of attention. She had her briefcase open on her lap, and there were two screens lit up on the inside, along with a handful of control tabs. She was running her drones, I realised – more with headware than fingers, from the way her eyes went in and out of focus.

Sturgeon brought me up to date. "Half a dozen attack drones latched onto us five minutes ago," he said, eyes fixed on Cormoran's screens. "One of the engines took a hit but it's still going."

"I can tell that," I said without much patience. There was another cracking report from the blind space outside the hull. From Cormoran's twitchy smile it was one of theirs, not one of ours. "This a hunter pack?"

"Just flak," Sturgeon said, meaning raiders set on autopilot and released in the general direction of our side, rather than tracking us down in particular. Just bad luck then, but Cormoran was more than equal to the challenge. Human-led is better than automatic still, in most fields. Her drones would have their own hair-trigger decision-making software, but she was feeding them a strategy moment to moment, keeping them unpredictable and managing the hacking war that must be going on between the little flying machines. It took her ten more minutes to strike out all of the enemy, using just two of her own. I guess that meant we could rely on her right up until the moment she sold us out.

A COUPLE HOURS after, we were being offloaded right where the 96th had its mobile command post. Orders had outstripped us, so that while there were all sorts of prickly officer types just dying to know who the hell we were, our corporate credentials meant they didn't get to ask, and there was an unmarked M1000 Trojan with my name on it, a nice compact ride with reinforced tyres and armor plate, and a minigun up top that Franken was instantly all over.

"Lovely, reliable rides, the Trojans," Franken said, letting it hang there.

"Their only drawback is that, when you're inside one, you feel like a dick," Sturgeon came back, right ahead of Lawes's. "It's what soldiers get into just before they get fucked." It's a testament to how some people just don't think it through before they name stuff.

The Onboard was loaded with our maps already, showing us where the Scion's signal had given out.

"This won't take us far," Lawes warned us. "Once we're out on our own any vehicle just draws attention. You can never mask the heat signature of something like this, and the partisans will have rockets and drones all over us the moment they guess who we are. And the terrain is a bloody bastard. You're a sitting duck on the road, and off the road, most of it's still forest, can you believe that? Like it's the bloody Middle Ages out here."

"Worse," Cormoran put in. She had her briefcase open again, and for a long moment I couldn't even work out what was on her screens. Then it started animating, frame by stilted frame, and I worked out that some parts of what I was seeing were a satellite view. The vast majority of what should have been contested Swedish soil was smeared with roiling dark clouds that obscured any sight we might have had of what the enemy was doing.

"Seriously," Sturgeon hissed, "what *is* that?"

"Is that the flies?" Lawes asked gloomily.

"Yeah." Cormoran gave us a bright look. "Gentlemen, this is a gift from the Finns. They breed these little bugs, midges, they chip 'em and ship 'em, and every so often the Nords release a batch. There are millions of the little critters each time, and they basically just block the view of our satellites – and we can't see a thing – no one can. So every time our forces advance, we're going in blind. Makes for all kinds of fun."

"They bite?" Franken asked uneasily. We were all thinking it: mosquitos, disease, some kind of Finnish lab-grown plague that zeroed in on the stars and stripes.

"Not yet," Lawes told us. "Jolly thought though, ain't it?"

The 96th were moving out that day, so we synced our helmet HUDs, got in our Trojan and tagged along. Scuttlebutt said light resistance – drone intel put the national Nord forces pulling back, but everyone reckoned they'd have left mines or mechanicals or something for us to have fun with. I had Franken drive and we found a place toward the back of the convoy. Sturgeon patched into the 96th's comms and we listened to what seemed like every individual soldier pinging us to try and work out who the hell we were and why they were letting us come to the party. Our corporate credentials were obviously suitably imposing. Nobody pinged us twice.

The 96th had their own drone wing out scouring the land ahead, and Cormoran was keeping her toys in their box. A squad of jets went screaming over once, but the fly-screen up above, which blocked the satellites and dulled the sun, had a trick of fouling jet intakes and abrading rotors; air support would be patchy at best.

There was an attack. Of course there was an attack.

I remember in Canada it was civilized warfare. There were skirmishes and shoot-outs; we took towns and villages, and we froze our asses off. We went head to head with the Canuck troops and the French troops and some severely tough Russians that nobody told us were there, and our Scions and theirs stomped about and played their own games with each other, and we tried to stay out of the way. That's war, and when we'd pacified a region, they knew it, and stayed pacified. It's not exactly the worst fate in the world, to have a few corporations putting drilling rigs and mines and sawmills on your land. It brings in money and jobs and solid libertarian values, and if you work hard, like they say, then you'll get paid. But the Nords didn't see it that way.

So, the attack. First off, everything stopped, because the lead scout vehicles had got bogged down. This was nothing natural – the retreating Nords had gone in for some serious improvised irrigation and suddenly we were looking at a crapton of swampland that hadn't been there a couple of days ago, and hadn't looked like anything to write home about when the drones overflew it. This wasn't the first time for this trick, and so the advance scouts were already converting their vehicles for amphibious work. What it did mean, though, was that everyone stopped. No prizes for guessing what came next.

Cormoran's briefcase lit up like the Fourth of July, all these alarms and lights, and then there were rockets coming at us. The Nords – probably Lawes's partisan irregulars – were in the trees and upslope to the south. They were a mile off at least, but they had a whole mess of handheld anti-armor kit, the cheap disposable stuff you could get for a song these days. You couldn't aim them for crap, and I reckon at least half must have gone wide of the entire convoy, but someone had gone on a serious shopping spree to kit out this bunch because everywhere was exploding at random. We had a front seat view of it from inside the Trojan – every camera was just showing us flash-bang and the air full of sprays of dirt, clods of earth being chucked around. Cormoran was trying to get her drones clear for a better picture of what was going on, but from her face I guess she didn't fancy her chances – there was just too much crap being thrown about for clear flying.

"Is this it?" I asked. "This can't be it," because it was all sound and fury out there, but the rockets weren't making much headway against the armor of the transports; we got bounced around, but hell if they were actually getting through to us.

Then we saw a vehicle ahead of us – it was a big Powell Defender transport, a score of men inside and it just leapt sideways with a flash so bright the cameras cut out for a second. Sturgeon was listening intently to the comms chatter. "Limpets," he reported, eyes wide.

"How the fuck are *they* getting drones through this shit?" Franken demanded.

"Because they're slow and they only need to drop them on us," from Cormoran.

"Disembark," Sturgeon relayed.

"Fuck that," was Franken's thought. I was in two minds. The rocket barrage, horribly inaccurate as it was, was slackening as the Nords burned through their toys. If a Limpet found the Trojan and latched on, it would burn us up quicker than the Powell had gone. And Limpet drones wouldn't be targeting men.

I went up into the little shell turret of the Trojan and got behind the gun, cameras giving me a 360 view of the field around us. The bigger armor was already retaliating, sending salvos off toward the partisans' positions. The transports were mostly yakking out their troops, men sprinting for cover or scanning the skies. I saw a Limpet coming it, like a bumblebee the size of my head, and picked it from the air with a quick burst of fire. A couple of our cars were gone – the air now getting thick with smoke as well as the last of the pattering dirt thrown up by the rockets, but we were taking back the initiative. Overhead, someone was risking a gunship, hovering and tilting above with its guns spitting sporadically. I hoped they were watching out for the fly-swarm if it suddenly dropped on our heads.

I heard Sturgeon shout out something from below. I didn't know it, but we'd had another gunship out there, and it had just set fire to a mile-long strip of forest to the south to try and dislodge the rocket-men. Then *something* had got it – it caused the same sort of devastation crashing down as it had when it was up and spraying phosphorus – and that *something* was coming for us.

"Oi, Sergeant!" from Lawes. "I reckon this is where we make our move."

"We're in the middle of a fight," I yelled back to him.

"Not our fight, remember? Higher calling, eh?" I swear sometimes Lawes just sounded like Dick Van Dyke to spite me.

Then company arrived, filling a big part of the sky. Because the fly-swarm didn't stop the *Nords* putting stuff in the air.

"*That*'s something you don't see every day," Cormoran said, sounding more impressed than I'd like.

"Move us out," I told Franken, sending a best-fit course to the driver's panel.

Cruising in at treetop height was probably the biggest gunship anyone had ever managed to get in the air. In Canada they'd had three of them across the whole front, and they were called something like Jodorowskys. Of course just being big didn't actually count for a whole deal, but they were built with that modern Slavic approach to engineering, all redundancy and hard-wearing components and no regard whatsoever for looking pretty. They took a lot of pounding before gravity took offence and yanked them down to earth.

This one was coming in all guns blazing – a blistering wall of counter-munitions fire to lock down the crap we were launching at it, and then its own ordnance bursting free of that firestorm to lance in at the transports. The incoming fire was focusing on the infantry transports, not the armor; they knew that armor took towns but men held them. That was today's war all over, though. These days, men were the cheapest part of any national army, the bit that was most easily replaced, least easily repurposed by the enemy, most easily forgiven when everyone shook hands over the treaty table.

Everyone was scattering now – the transports were nothing more than targets for the firepower the gunship was turning out. Those who were out and free to run around were getting cut up too, but it was incidental – they simply didn't rank highly enough as targets.

Franken was guiding us out from between a couple of tanks, both of which were incandescent as they threw all they had at the Jodorowsky. If we'd had a corporate detachment with us we'd probably already have won, but these days the main line army just doesn't get the best toys.

"You never said there were so many Russians here, Lawes!" I yelled.

"You ever know a fight in the last ten years that wasn't

bloody crawling with White Russians?" he hollered back, and that was true enough.

Our own remaining gunship had pulled out, or at least I couldn't see it and I hadn't seen it go down. I was torn. Orders were that this wasn't our business. But these were our people. It didn't feel right just to skip out on them, for all we couldn't do much to help.

That was when the cavalry arrived. I hadn't realized we even had Scions with the 96th until three of them came vaulting through the smoke. Something I'd seen a hundred times before, sure, but you never get used to it. You always catch your breath, if you've got even a sliver of soul left in you. They were like gods: human figures head and shoulders over the soldiers around them, made of gleaming silver and gold and darkly menacing black steel. And they *were* gods, in a way. This was what human ingenuity could achieve, when price was no object. The corporations wouldn't shell out to give us common grunts that sort of protection, but it was only the best when their sons wanted to play soldier.

They were unleashing a barrage of firepower at the Jodorowsky, and suddenly the tables had – not just turned, but been completely flipped over. The weapons built into those beautiful shiny shells cut through all the counter-ordnance the gunship could muster, striking strings of explosions off the enemy hull. When the Jodorowsky replied in kind, the Scions were briefly enveloped in fire and shrapnel, but when the flare cleared, two of them still stood, and the third was getting back to his feet. I almost expected him to brush his metal chassis down like he was dusting off a tuxedo.

The soldiers around them hadn't been so lucky, of course. Bitter thought.

We were pulling out by then, heading off and ignoring the pings and queries of the column officers who wanted to know what the hell our business was. Behind us, I saw the Jodorowsky falter in the sky for a moment – as if physics had suddenly served it with a cease-and-desist, but then it was backing away, ponderously thundering upward, driven away by three boys who had shinier suits and richer folks than its pilots did.

And then we were clear of it all. Sturgeon had filleted the scout intel about the impromptu swampland the Nords had thrown up, and luckily it looked as though we could bee-line it for Cousin Jerome's last known whereabouts without getting ourselves bogged down.

"Got one question, though," because of course Sturgeon always had questions. "What the hell was our guy doing so far in front of the fighting?"

Somehow none of us had thought to ask that before. I came down from the turret and saw looks passing between them that spoke eloquently of just how none of them really trusted each other. Oh, Franken and me and Sturgeon were a team, but the other two were loners. I'd pegged Lawes as someone who very greatly valued his own skinny little hide, and Cormoran... Why did I think that if only one of us got out of this alive, it would be Cormoran?

"Spying, maybe?" Franken suggested, making me realize that the long pause on his part had actually been because he was thinking. It was a good call – Scions did a lot of espionage work, mostly industrial. Cousin Jerome could have been off stealing Nord secrets when they zapped him with this new anti-Scion thing of theirs. Maybe that was the actual secret he'd been after.

"Just get us there," I told Franken. "Cormoran, you're our eyes. Lawes... what do we need you for exactly?"

The Englishman gave me his rat's grin. "I don't know about your Scion, Sarge, but I've been kicking about in this bloody country since before the war. Think of me as your multi-tool, to get you out of whatever you get into."

"A tool for every occasion, right," I agreed, which was wasted on him.

We had a jolting and uncomfortable time of it for the next hour or so, which was fine by me. I'll take 'not being shot at' over 'dead in comfort' any time. "So do the Nords know we're here?" I asked Lawes, partway in.

"Someone will know we're here," he confirmed, in a sour mood. He had tried to light up inside the Trojan three times, by then, and after the stench of his uniquely horrible tobacco had brought the rest of us close to vomiting, I'd ended up taking his tin off him. "Thing is," he went on, "it's not like they're all talking to each other, over there. Between the initial bombing runs and the ECM slap-fight last year, most of the comms infrastructure's buggered, so they're basically down to carrier pigeons over half the country. So maybe some partisan cell or a corporate scouting detachment's seen this one US scout car lost in the woods, but who're they going to tell? We'll only know about it if they come and give us a kick. Which they will, soon enough."

"Gentlemen," Cormoran told us abruptly. "I see them."

She was flying her drones high, hanging them just below the fly swarm's lower reaches, spying out the trees ahead. Pure visual showed nothing, and they had set camp with a mess of heat-baffling tarps above them, but there was still just enough signature leaking out to show us someone was there. Mind you, Cormoran was corporate; she had superior gear.

"They've seen us?"

"Probably." Cormoran shrugged. "They're not moving on us with anything mechanical, but they might send men out." Sending men out was like trying to map out a minefield with a long stick: nobody cared what happened to the stick and you could always get another one.

"Go round?" Sturgeon suggested. If they were going to show an interest in us, that was unlikely to help. Franken had throttled down our own heat, running as cold as possible, but the Trojan was still going to stand out.

Lawes was peering at the images. "They got drones out?"

Cormoran skimmed back through images on one screen and pulled up a shot of a silvery disc-looking flier glimpsed between trees. At Lawes' behest she zoomed in and then more until it filled the screen – fuzzy and blurred but still visible for all that.

Lawes gave a thoughtful grunt and settled back. "Shanks's

pony," he suggested, which apparently meant go on foot if you were English.

But we weren't ready for that yet, or I wasn't. I had Franken take a detour, and Cormoran keep a long-distance eye on what the enemy were doing, whoever the enemy were. We crept on at a snail's pace, cool and quiet as possible, and nobody stirred from the camp under our drones' watchful gaze.

I took a nap for a while and – as happens far too often in this line of work – the fighting woke me. Not an attack from outside, but the entirety of my team trying to kill each other right there in front of me.

CHAPTER THREE

I AM ASHAMED to admit that I thought *Mind-control gas!* first off, even though the Trojan's filters would have kept anything like that out, and nobody had used gas weapons against military targets since the Luobu debacle. Weapons that can be screwed over by a change in the weather are never worth the bother.

It wasn't mind-control gas – if there even was such a thing – it was just my dumbass squad being fuckwits.

Sturgeon was already on his ass with his hand pressed to his temple. He hadn't actually been in the fight, I discovered later. Franken had been going for Lawes, and had elbowed Sturgeon in the head by accident as he lunged as if his body was so conditioned to slapping his comrade around that it had suffered a targeting error. Lawes had a knife out, and was backed right into the back corner of the Trojan, half-hiding behind our gear. Cormoran was nursing a cut hand, which suggested she and Franken had become unlikely allies.

I asked them all to tell me what was going on, which sounds a damn sight more polite than it came out at the time.

"That little fucker's sold us out!" Franken yelled, tensed to spring for Lawes.

"Oi, listen –" the Englishman started, but I shouted him down.

"Cormoran, report."

The corporate gave me a somewhat mutinous look but complied. "Your man there caught an outgoing signal. Lawes was talking with the enemy."

"Just hear me out –" Lawes tried again, but I snapped, "How long for?"

"No idea," Sturgeon got out, grimacing. "He was encrypted on some weirdass short range frequency." There was a beauty of a bruise coming up about his eye. "I was just messing with comms. I was bored."

I had my pistol out and at Lawes without really thinking about it. A shot inside the Trojan could do a lot of damage if it starting bouncing around, but I reckon it wouldn't do half as much if Lawes ate it first.

"Jesus Christ, will you just listen?" the Englishman demanded, and then flinched back when Franken half went for him.

"Don't blaspheme," I warned. "He doesn't like it."

Lawes' eyes bugged out a bit. "Seriously?"

"First Church of Christ Libertarian is *very* serious about taking His name in vain," I confirmed. It was odd to see that rattle Lawes more than the gun, but they were weird about religion where he came from. "Now how about you start talking?"

"That lot out there, I know them," Lawes got out quickly. "They're Nord corporates, not the nationals. That means they're not fighting us."

"Plenty of Nord corps are fighting us," Sturgeon snapped.

"Not them – look, seriously, when you lot first weighed in here it was only 'cos you were asked in by a bunch of Euro-based multinationals who were getting their stuff nicked, right? Now, I agree that once the real fighting started, a lot of the Eurocorps had to at least pretend they were fighting for the national interest, but most of them are just clockwatching. After all, when the war's done, they'll all be best friends again, right? This lot are Skaalmed special forces, and what they're mostly about is watching over their corporate holdings until it's safe to go back to business as usual."

"So?"

"So they won't fight us, for starters," Lawes pressed. "So they can take us right where we want to go, escort us there – the partisans and whatever other fuckery they have, they won't go for us if we're with 'their' people," and he did that thing with his fingers for the 'their'.

"And why would they do this?" I asked him.

He gave me a sickly smile. "I know them; they know

me. We've done business together before. There are plenty Skaalmed boys owe me a favor."

For a moment the situation balanced on Lawes' knife edge. "Cormoran," I said. "Get yourself patched up."

"Already on it." And of course she had some crap in her that let her heal fast. Somebody had *invested* in Cormoran.

"Okay," and I lowered the gun. "Last question, Lawes. Why not just *tell* us?"

I caught his face naked then; there was no subterfuge in it, none of that ratty cunning, just complete surprise. He'd never thought to; it just wasn't in his nature. I guessed he'd been playing his own games out here for so long that he'd run out of people to confide in years ago.

"If you want to go off-script some time, you clear it with me," I told him, "or I will serve you to Franken. You got that?"

He nodded, servile as you like, but I wondered. I wondered what sort of business he did with Nord corps, and just how much that was going to bite us in the ass. If we were going to go eat breakfast with the Nords at Lawes's invitation, I was sure as hell going to keep close enough to snap his scrawny neck if things went bad.

I had him put me in touch with the Nord commander, and she and I – it threw me a little that she was a she and maybe it shouldn't have – had a little chat. It was the first test of our translation software, too, so I let the woman's Swedish wash over me, with all its improbable vowels and weirdass inflections, while a pleasantly urbane male voice spoke over it, giving me the Nord's deal with a Californian accent. This was Överste Rurisksdottir of Skaalmed AB's Asset Protection Division. Skaalmed were big business, and so Rurusksdottir probably had serious hardware at her disposal, and sufficient Swede cred to warn off the locals. If Lawes could be trusted, then his deal sounded good.

I wanted to ask for orders right then, but trying to hail the 96th's column might give us away to other enemies, and might not go down well with Skaalmed either. Besides, unless Rich Ted Speling was anywhere within earshot, there wasn't exactly anyone who *could* give me orders.

So I trusted Lawes, in the end. I promised myself not to make a habit of it. We went to break bread with the Nords.

ÖVERSTE RURISKSDOTTIR WAS one of those women who drew your eye whenever she walked into the room. It might have been the enormous chrome exoskeleton. She was a Skaalmed Scion, but whatever else she might have been, she was sure as hell trying to connect with her inner Viking. There were spiky runes edging the plates of her shell, and she had an actual hammer – something it would have taken four men to lift – magnet-locked to her back. There were horns on her headpiece, and I leant over to Sturgeon and told him that if he was going to pass some comment about Vikings and history and horned helmets – he'd done it three times since we set foot in Nord country – then no power on earth would save him from the consequences. And for once he kept his mouth shut.

Most Scions are built well enough to put over body

language when they want to, and Ruriskdottir's suggested strongly that she wasn't impressed with us. The Skaalmed detachment numbered about a hundred, but they were toting some serious gear: not just the disc-shaped drones we'd seen, but some miniature armor that could switch from tracks to legs for the rough terrain, and packed considerably more punch than our Trojan. They had mechs, too – that stilty Netherlands type that look like Martian war machines and were such a pain in the ass in Mexico. One of them was active and patrolling, and every time it passed it stopped and stared at us with the cluster of camera eyes clumped in the center of its round body. A Skaalmed logo flanked them on the left, and the red arrows of Ruud, the manufacturer, on the right. And a nasty pair of gun barrels below, which kind of dominated my attention.

As for the troops themselves, they were neat and disciplined and ready, and edgier than I was expecting. Corporate elites, with all their fancy gear, you don't imagine them being jumpy, but this lot kept their eyes on the forest and cast a broad net with their drones. About one in three were women, which was an odd thing to see these days. I'd served with plenty of women in my time, but back home the creed of Christ Libertarian had very strong views about a woman's place, and it wasn't on the battlefield. Congress hadn't made it illegal for women to sign up, but current regs didn't make it easy for them.

The Överste and I had a carefully phrased conversation through our respective translation software.

"You won't tell me what you're coming out here for," she

told me. Like all Scions, her mech body could stand still forever while she reclined inside. That meant I had to stand too, if I wanted her take me seriously. We were at one edge of the camp, and I took in the darkening treescape, listening to the faint hums of the drones, the whine of insects and the staccato chatter of birds.

"We've got somewhere we need to be," I explained. "If you're sharing, any intel would be appreciated. If we're allies."

She made a grating sound that I recognized a moment later as a sigh. "I've not known what we are from day to day for about a year, Sergeant Regan. Back when we kicked all this off, they told me it would be over within three months of your lot being invited in. The socialists would fold under popular pressure, they said. Nobody thought the *people* would back them to the hilt – until way after they would have preferred to surrender, in fact. The Swedish army is still in the field because it's become a point of national pride, of national *identity* even, that we fight. And nobody thought the Finns would back us. And nobody thought it would be such a god-damned *cause celebre* in the Euro-union either." And I have no idea whether she actually said that bit in French or whether my translator was getting above itself.

"That must make it awkward for you," I said diplomatically.

She whacked one immense fist into the armored palm of the other hand, making me jump back, and drawing the startled attention of my fellows. It was just that, though, just the one motion, and the danger ebbed after a moment.

"If it were me, just me, Ada Rurisksdottir of Sandviken, then I would take up a gun and fight for my country," she told me in the male Californian tones of my software. "But my family fought long and hard to get on the board and I have a duty to our shareholders. Our shareholders are not even majority Swedish. So we sit out here and wait to see how the arguments go, over in Stockholm. If the socialists continue to be stubborn, then we are halfway your allies. If things go another way, perhaps tomorrow we are your enemies."

"But for now?" I pressed.

"For now? I have spoken to your pet English. We help you get where you need, and don't ask questions. I will give you Intel and a clear route to your coordinates, and a best guess at what's in the way."

"Who controls the country between here and there?"

"Nobody controls anything," she told me bitterly. "You're on the shores of the Vättern by then. There was some serious fighting there – your advance forces, the nationals and the partisans. This was before the lines crystallised, when you were still just dropping men and mechs wherever you liked. For a month there was even a boat war up there on the lake. There was a big factory at Tunnerstad on the island there, someone's research facility. I never did find out what they were doing there, but someone bombed it and then everything went straight to hell. Now you've got freelance Euro marauders that way, and cells of locals fighting everyone and everything, and... worse."

I knew precisely who 'worse' meant: the same faction

that had gifted the satellite view with its pest problem, and half the Nord war veterans with their nightmares, to hear people talk about it. "They're active up there, are they?"

"That was where they first showed people what they'd been cooking up in their labs over the border," Rurisksdottir confirmed grimly. "Look up how the Vättern boat war ended, if you don't believe me. Nobody had any idea, before that."

We spent a night on Skaalmed's hospitality, while Sturgeon and Cormoran looked over their intel and planned our next move. Why had Cousin Jerome been out on the banks of the Vättern? Probably not for his health. Had there been industrial secrets hidden in the ruined research facility? Had he just been some privileged kid who got lost?

Did the Finns have a weapon that killed Scions?

WE GOT TO within a day's easy walk of the coordinates before we lost the Trojan. To be honest I don't think any of us had expected it to last so long.

Cormoran had her drones flying wide, which gave us a little advance warning when the enemy tried to bring one of them down with a barrage of rockets. While she was wrestling with that, Franken was taking us away, but the drone flying ahead of us reported more heat signatures – mechanicals suddenly powering up as we got close. We'd driven into a trap.

Even then we might have got out of the net: Cormoran

had given us a chance, and Franken took it with both hands. We were off-road, though, and the country out that way was riddled with little lakes and streams that suddenly opened up from between the trees like mouths. The ground was unpredictably soft between them – something the drones just couldn't know beforehand. One moment we were looking good to get clean away, the next we were slewing sideways toward a dark expanse of water of unknown depth, half our wheels churning mud. Franken wrestled us clear the first time with judicious jockeying of the gas, but there just wasn't a straight path of dry ground to be had anywhere we turned. I don't know whether the locals had been damming and flooding or whether it was just the land itself we were fighting, but the enemy caught up to us just as we plowed into another mire and began to flay the armor from our right side.

Trojans are, as they say, designed for deep insertion. This meant they were designed to last long enough under fire to give the occupants a chance to get out. Lawes took the turret this time, swinging the minigun about to give an answer to all those urgent questions the enemy were asking us. I hunched by Cormoran to get a drone's eye view of who was after us. As I'd half-guessed, they were Ruuds, that same model of tripod mech that Rurisksdottir had been packing. Probably she hadn't betrayed us – you saw machines like these wherever the fighting went; they were reliable and none too expensive.

This lot were tooled up with the squat box of a rocket battery, and a minigun that wasn't much inferior to ours.

I saw two of them stalking forward, broad, padded feet managing the treacherous ground better than our wheels had. They were concentrating on emptying rockets into the flank of the Trojan – the wheels there had already been shredded, but the armor was holding.

One of them was abruptly cut down, a leg scythed away and then a jagged line of holes chewed across its compact body by our gun. Then our chassis shuddered, and Lawes dropped down out of the turret, cursing. That marked the end of the Trojan's ability to defend itself.

We were ready to go by then. Sturgeon popped the side-hatch away from the Ruuds, and we crashed out into shin-deep muddy water. Lawes had the opportunity to utter a cry of despair as another of the Ruuds rose from the black lake ahead of us, close enough to poke with a flagstaff. I looked into its lenses as water ran from it and the barrel of its minigun spun up. I swear the bastard was gloating.

A bright flash lit it up, and pieces of mangled weapon pod were flying overhead to rattle from the Trojan's abused hull. Then another, so the machine staggered sideways, trying to get its launcher in line as we lurched and stumbled along our doomed transport's side. Then Franken pumped a grenade into it, right where one of its legs met the body. His aim was spot-on textbook perfect, shattering the vulnerable joint and pitching the entire machine backward to be lost in the water.

One of Cormoran's drones spun and hovered where it had been – the source of the initial hit. It was like a dragonfly as long as your arm, but it must have been packing some serious weaponry somewhere.

"There's still one out there!" Sturgeon yelled, and even as he did, something gave on the Trojan's far side and the vehicle shuddered a foot further toward the lake with the impact. We lurched out from its shadow shooting, guided by the eyes of Cormoran's drones. The last remaining Ruud was already chattering at us with its gun, and I swear Franken never came closer to being killed in his life. The Ruud was already reeling from a pair of drone strikes, though, oily smoke issuing from somewhere inside its cracked carapace. I finished it off myself, three rounds into its lenses, and then another three and another, pushing deeper and deeper until I hit something vital.

When it was down, we crouched in the mud, behind the trees, and we waited. Cormoran had her briefcase before her, spiraling her drones out further and further, looking for any more teeth of the trap that were coming late to the party. When let loose without human operators, Ruuds use a net mind – trigger one and you trigger them all. At the same time, they're not programmed for suicide. We'd just trashed three of them, so the rest of the pack might write us off as too tough to take on. Probably they'd already reported us to whoever set them out here, if they even had a live human contact any more. Autonomous mechs without a handler to shut them down were as dangerous as forgotten minefields after the fighting had finished. That was one reason we didn't tend to use them, but nobody else seemed to see it that way.

We let Cormoran do her thing for an hour before anyone was willing to call the all clear. After that, while Sturgeon and I kept an eye out, Franken set about scalping. It was a habit of his, and occasionally a useful one. With surprising deftness he took his tools to the Ruud I'd downed, and dug until he had isolated and removed its brain.

"You have got to be kidding me." Lawes watched in fascinated horror as Doctor Franken performed his surgery. "Is he going to wear it about his neck like a trophy or something?"

I nodded to Sturgeon, who never needed an excuse to show people he knew stuff they didn't.

"Best defense against mechs like this," he explained smugly. "Their net mind is always reaching out to reincorporate missing elements, so we'll kill this one's transmitter, but leave it receiving. When its buddies turn up looking for it, we'll know. Also, Franken likes to play with them."

"Is that right?" Lawes was torn between being disturbed and impressed. It felt good to know a trick the Englishman didn't.

"They talk," Franken grunted, finishing off. "I'm gonna hook Freddo here to a translator and see what's going on in his little mind." He held up the mech's brain, ragged with severed wiring.

Sturgeon kept his eyes on Lawes' face. "The AI's pretty complex, with the Ruud models," he explained with relish. "Sometimes they beg."

Lawes' eyes flicked between the two of them. "That's cobblers," he decided.

Sturgeon and Franken grinned in unison, best friends now they had someone else to annoy.

"We should move," Cormoran said quietly at my shoulder. Being who she was, she could have tried to pull corporate rank on me, I guess, so I appreciated her discretion. Of course, whether Franken or the rest would have followed her orders is another question.

It didn't take any time at all for us to declare the Trojan out of the fight. It would take more than a puncture repair kit to get it moving again. That done, I set my three subordinates to clear out everything we could use while I took Cormoran aside. From the way she was standing about, I could see she had something to say that was just for me.

"You strike me as a smart man, Sergeant," she told me.

I regarded her doubtfully. "You've got low standards."

"Well I came in with Lawes, so what do you expect?"

I couldn't stop a smile at that one. "So what is it I'm missing, is that what you're going to tell me?"

"I've seen your records, Sergeant: long service, but it's not exactly all medals and commendations."

"So?" Of course she'd seen all our records. The army didn't say no when the big corporations came asking.

"So haven't you wondered why it's you here, and not a corp team?"

"They don't like to get their hands dirty?" I shrugged. Inside, I felt a stab of unease. It was a good question, and I didn't like to think I'd bought into that Rich Ted/Poor Ted thing so much that it had gone under the radar.

"We're trying to get back one of their own: a son of the corporate families," she pointed out, keeping her voice low.

"What expense would they spare, exactly?"

"You tell me," I shot back, harder than I'd intended. "You're one of theirs, after all. You're no grunt. So whatever we're actually being sent to do, you'll be all right."

"Is that what you think?" Her face had closed up again, putting distance between us, even though she didn't move a step. I was going to deny it, just a knee-jerk, but then I didn't, and she nodded. "That is what you think, then? I'm going to sell you."

"And cheap." I shrugged. "Nothing we haven't seen before. The army gets the crap jobs. The army gets sent in whenever the corps need meat for the grinder. That's what Sturgeon says." It was pretty much just the tip of the iceberg of what Sturgeon said, but it was about as far as I would follow him.

"Yeah, well." I didn't see the tension across her shoulders until she let them sag. "Happens that way sometimes. Not this time. I'm as fucked as the rest of you, believe me."

We stared at each other for a moment, and I heard a clatter and a whine of fans from inside the Trojan, and Sturgeon chattering happily about whatever they'd just woken up.

"If it helps, I figured they were sending us because they didn't know what the hell ate the Speling boy." I guessed she wouldn't think of him as Cousin Jerome. "They aren't going to risk another Scion, or maybe anything expensive. So I did think of it that much." Not as much as I should have done.

She shrugged again. "Keep on thinking that. Maybe it'll turn out to be true."

Then our three brave salvagers turned up, and they had a pet. It was one of the BigBug load-carriers that we so seldom got to play with, a headless, squat, six-legged robot that would obligingly cart all our gear around for us. We loaded it up with rations and ammo and tents and all the rest of the salvageable gear from the Trojan. Then we set off on foot because, while I can't speak for the other two, we of the 203rd can be stubborn to a bloody-minded fault when we set out minds to it.

CHAPTER FOUR

CORMORAN HAD HER drones out as our long-range eyes, and Lawes turned out to be a surprisingly good pathfinder who kept us from getting our new boots too wet (the spares we'd all changed into after we got dumped on the lakeshore). The soundtrack for that trek was a constant muttering complaint coming from Franken's direction, though not actually from Franken. This was the brain he'd taken from the Ruud, which he'd patched through his translator into a little earphone speaker. If you leant in close, you could hear the bastard thing trying to report in that easy Californian accent, calling out for its absent siblings and then – I swear this is true – cussing out Franken like you wouldn't believe, threatening him with physical violence and Euro-law prosecution for what he'd done to it. I don't know much about battlefield AI, but I reckoned those Ruudboys had been out there a long while to get that glitchy and personality-filled.

We were due more than our share of shit, that journey, but it was the flies that started the next round. It wasn't as if our journey had been insect-free, but after four hours or so we started to realize that the air was getting busy with them, the dark beneath the trees flurrying like static with the blur of little wings. Sturgeon was casting anxious looks upward, as if that whole satellite-blocking fly-screen was just going to descend on us like weather. What tipped me off more was Cormoran: she had her briefcase on her back, and was flying her drones with a little handheld console and her headware, but from the look of it, it wasn't doing the trick.

"Give me five, Sergeant?" she asked.

I nodded, signalled Sturgeon to keep watch, and Cormoran opened up her case and tried to sort her toys out.

"What's up?" I asked her.

"I'm losing contact," she told me. "The distance at which I can actually link to them is shrinking as we travel."

"It's a power problem?"

"I charged up all the batteries from the Trojan; they should be good for days yet. It's some sort of interference…"

I swatted at the low whine of a fly, then examined my palm critically. If I'd be expecting to see tiny spilled microcircuitry for guts, I was disappointed. "Is it these bastards?"

I wanted her to laugh that off, but she just frowned.

"Is it the satellite screen come to take a look at us?" I pressed.

"I don't think so, but something from the same labs. Look."

She showed me some readings on her case screen. Suffice to say they were too technical for me to make much of them, which must have shown on my face.

"They carry a charge – the flies. Each on its own is nothing, but enough of them together and they just… cause interference, screw with our comms and my drones. I'm not going to be able to keep a proper watch – right now I can't send anything more than about a hundred yards before I lose the link, and I don't want to trust them on automatic, that's too easy to fool. If it gets worse…"

"We could get zapped by these things?"

She really wanted to dismiss that one, but then she gave another of her shrugs. "Fuck knows, Sergeant," was her frank appraisal of the situation.

Lawes got us to the edge of the Vättern after that, where all the fighting had been. Intel was patchy, so I had Sturgeon pop out all the warning tech we could get – Geiger counter, chem-hazard, everything. We were getting toward dusk then, just when we'd found some country that was no use whatsoever for hiding in. We were exposed out at the water's edge, with the dark bulk of the island hunching up the horizon across the water. There had been a lab or something there, Rurisksdottir had said. I decided that I didn't want to go find out, and looking back I'm glad that was one command decision I got to stand by.

After a brief conference with our expat Englishman, we pressed on alongside the water, more and more jumpy, picking up pace as the daylight left us, the BigBug labouring patiently in our wake.

We found some little town that had been a harbour before everything kicked off. It looked as though it would have been a nice little tourist retreat or retirement place, stuck on a little strip of low ground between the water and the trees. They'd fought over it for weeks, Lawes said. All those nice suburban homes and gardens trampled by men and mechs and Scions, torn up by shells and the treads of tanks. And for what? Nobody was there now, not our guys, not their guys. Whatever strategic objective had been served by dropping men and machines onto the shore of the Vättern had long since become obsolete. Or else everyone's guys had been driven off. Like Lawes said, like Rurisksdottir had said, there were more than two sides to this war.

We pitched camp in the broken shell of a big, ruined quad – might have been a school once, or some government office or just a really fancy house. It gave us cover and plenty of ways out if we had to bug out, which was what mattered. We got attacked in the night, too. There was a hectic twenty minutes of gunfire enlivened by one really badly aimed Molotov cocktail, followed by about two hours of occasional potshots at us. This broken place, this wrecked gravel shadow of a town, still had its residents. It's one thing you learn in this job: some people won't ever leave home. Some people will cling on no matter what; they've got nowhere else to go.

We all had night-sights, and we had Cormoran's drones. From the images she captured, I don't think the locals had anything other than a handful of scavenged assault rifles and a grab-bag of hunting weapons. I gave orders to scare them off, but there's no accounting for bad luck, and there must have been at least a couple who ducked late or took the wrong left. They weren't soldiers; they weren't even the partisans we'd been warned of. I don't exactly count it as a grand victory over the Nords. I think they might have been after our rations as much as our blood.

Come first light, we were all eager to get going, because the alternative would be to stay and see if parts of the rubble-jagged landscape would suddenly resolve themselves into dead faces and outflung limbs.

We took to the treeline, moving parallel to the water's edge, as the interference drew Cormoran's drones closer and closer to us, until they were always a constant hovering presence or just perching on her shoulders. The robot brain kept up its muttering, which seemed to buck up Franken's spirits, if nobody else's.

There was a wrecked ship we saw, half-beached in the shallows. Like Rurisksdottir had said, there'd been a bit of a boat war on the Vättern. The wreck had been a compact gunship, and one of the turrets was still sticking one finger up at the sky. The grey armored hull had been shredded below the waterline, the damage revealed when it heeled over in final defeat. I'd never seen the like: the metal just snipped up and pulled open like someone had taken a pair of sharp pliers to a toy.

"There's probably some still alive in there," Lawes said glumly, nodding at the inky water.

"Some what?" I asked him.

"You didn't hear what the Finns brought, to clear everyone out? Crabs." Everyone was looking at him like he was mad, and he shook his head mournfully. "They just seeded the lake with them – little ones, when they did it – and the bloody things grew and grew – big as cars, someone told me. They just tore open anything that put out on the water – and any*one*." He chuckled, in that miserable English way of his. "Funny thing is, there was always supposed to be a monster in the Vättern – like Nessie, you know? – and now it's got more monsters than anyone knows what to do with."

"You made that up," Franken growled at him, but Lawes met his gaze without a flinch.

It was within an hour that we hit our coordinates. There were no giant crab attacks that I'm admitting to.

HALF AN HOUR later and we still didn't know much more. There had been a camp there – our man hadn't just been got strolling down the lovely crab-infested lakeshore. Lawes tried to piece the tracks together, but there was little enough to find given the time that had passed. The drones picked up more. Cormoran had some kind of scene-of-crime software she set up, and I got to peer at models of how things might have been based on the marks and prints and scars that had been left behind. A tent, she thought, and thermal baffling sheets – she'd pinpointed the attachment points on the trees nearby. Soil analysis showed where a heater had been sat, and by that time Lawes had turned up a couple of empty Nord ration packets, just scrappy films of foil, but they told a story. A small team had been parked here, waiting, and then our man had come along. And then he'd vanished off the map, somehow.

Cormoran set the drones on a spiral pattern, looking for a trail we could follow, but by then Lawes had found fresher prints. They should have been none of our business – they were clearly far more recent then whatever had happened to Cousin Jerome. What got us worried was that they came out of the lake.

None of us were happy with the idea, but once Lawes had shown them to us we couldn't doubt his conclusions. They must have been fresh that morning, and they were… How to describe them? They were almost human. Think about that: I'm not sure there's anything more frightening. Not mech tracks, not monsters. We could plainly see the imprint of toes, of fingers, but longer than they should have been. They put me in mind of werewolf movies.

"We need to move," Lawes decided. He looked at me with his big teeth bared, like a dog anxious to be let off the leash. "This is Finnish SpecOps. They could be here right now." And what was worse was, he was looking toward the water as though they might just be hanging there like drowned men, beneath the surface.

"Have we got anywhere to move to?" I demanded.

"Yes." Cormoran looked up from her open case. "I have a trail. Tracked vehicle, probably a converted PBV 5-series or similar." I had my helmet HUD call it up: a heavily armored car not a million miles from our Trojan. "It's faint," Cormoran went on. "We'll have to take it slow or we might just lose it altogether, but we've got something to follow. Heading inland, looks like."

All this time, Franken's stolen brain had kept up its mutinous grumbling – you just tuned it out after a while. Right then, though, even as Cormoran was calling her drones back, the translator's flawless Californian snapped out, "Oh you bastards are in for it now!"

Even though it couldn't reach out to them, the brain had felt the first electronic touch of its friends.

For a moment we just crouched there, weapons at the ready and listening, hearing nothing. Then Sturgeon and one of the drones caught the first heat signature through the trees at about the same time.

We got moving sharpish, skipping over terrain that was lumpy with rock and root and pocked by gaping craters that nature hadn't been able to mend. Behind us, the Ruuds would be striding forward, stilting over the terrain with their long legs. I'd seen them in action often enough to track their progress in my mind's eye. They looked awkward and teetering, but they could put in a hell of a turn of speed over rough ground.

Our heading was away from the water, because if we got caught in the open between the trees and the lake then we'd be dead meat on legs. Franken, bringing up the rear, turned to launch an incendiary in the general direction of the enemy every half minute or so, keeping them busy and screwing with their heat imaging.

"Can we sacrifice the Bug?" Cormoran asked, doggedly keeping pace with her case swinging in one hand.

I had a frantic going-on-holiday moment of trying to remember what we'd stowed where, what of the Bug's load we could reasonably carry. "Is this going to slow them or stop them?"

"Just slow."

"Free the gear and it's yours."

She was already in the Bug's systems, and it jettisoned its clasps and straps explosively, spilling duffle bags and tins and the tents over the forest floor. Everyone grabbed what they could – we'd be leaving a lot of hot meals behind us, and our next sleeping arrangements would be newly intimate. We ran on, and behind us the Bug wheeled nimbly on its six feet and then lumbered off into battle.

I didn't see what it did at the time, but Cormoran had drone footage she showed me later: the little carrier robot charging like a doomed knight toward the great stalking strides of the Ruuds. Something – one of Cormoran's somethings – meant they didn't flag it as a target until it was quite close, or perhaps they were just too fixated on us. It must have been within ten yards when the nearest of the trio of mechs stopped and started shooting at it. The valiant Bug lost two legs in that burst, but it could still hop about on the remaining four, and it closed the distance in a sudden mad rush. In my mind, it was screaming a battle cry.

It blew – the drone's cameras were just flat white for a second, and in the aftermath one of the Ruuds was down, and another was staggering and limping, one leg damaged and trailing. A half-dozen trees had been torn into as well – there was a matchwood-strewn crater where the Bug had been, with odds and pieces still pattering down.

I swear, if I knew that was a thing the Bugs could do, I'd not have gotten within twenty feet of one of them.

The last Ruud was still coming, in the drone's footage, and Cormoran was yelling that same news to me right then and there as we ran. I was weighing up the odds: probably we could turn and ambush it now, the five of us against a machine. Certainly we couldn't just keep running.

Then the forest ahead of us whomped into flames – abruptly the trees were a wall of fire, all that damp wood and earth seething and spitting and cracking in the instant inferno heat.

"That wasn't from the Ruud!" Sturgeon shouted.

We were already changing course, now running parallel to the trees' edge instead of away from it. Another incendiary shell exploded past us, lighting up a hundred yards of beach with flames that could burn underwater.

Lawes was swearing to himself. The rest of us were saving our energy for running. Except Cormoran, whose drones were obediently feeding her images of just what had run into us.

"White Walker!" she cried, and that's when our day got a whole lot worse.

Like Lawes said, if there's fighting, there's Russians. These days they're the premier mercenaries the world over: they don't quit and they're backed by enough money to make even a few of them a serious problem. This isn't the government, what they're calling the Red Russians now. This is what happened when that government finally went all out on those rich oligarchs and their families, took their property and drove them out to make them everybody else's problem. Some of them were legitimate businessmen and some were criminal families and some were former government types who had picked the wrong side. What they became, though, was a well-monied class of global exiles: the White Russians.

And of course, most of them just found gainful employment around the world, but you know what? In my trade I never got to meet that type. I got to meet representatives of the mercenary clans who had got out of Russia with their fortunes intact, enough to equip a private army well enough to go head-to-head with corporate special forces.

And of course the favored sons of these military exiles went to war, just like the sons of our great corporate clans. And, just as with them, they spared no expense. Except that while Rich Ted Speling or Överste Rurisksdottir had shells that could get through a decent-sized doorway, fit for a hostile takeover in the boardroom as well as a battlefield, the White Russians thought big. What came striding toward us through its own wall of fire was as tall as the trees, which it shouldered aside without difficulty. The White Walker was a brutalist, headless humanoid shape, with two arms low at the front for grabbing and crushing, and two more off its shoulders that were basically just enormous toyboxes of weapons. Its front was painted with a vastly complex coat of arms full of saints and horsemen and five different colors of eagle.

For a moment, the fire was messing with its instruments and it just stood there, receding behind us as we ran. Then it got intel from the Ruud and began following us, moving at a leisurely stomp that sent shockwaves through the ground to us and shivered the branches of the trees.

It was a Scion. We could fight men and we could fight mechs, but we had nothing that would touch it. Nobody had bought us that sort of firepower.

Sturgeon says – and I appreciate this is an odd time to be talking about what Sturgeon says, but it's crazy what goes through your head when you're running for your life – Sturgeon says that it's not even just that they're cheap. He says that they could give us common soldiers Scion-killer weapons if they wanted, but that would be putting the power in our hands. Scions fight Scions, like chess players play against chess players. We pawns are just here to get taken.

That's what Sturgeon says. Right then, with the White Walker rattling our teeth with each step, it was hard to argue with.

Another couple of incendiaries went over our heads and exploded five square yards of forest ahead and to the left; we were fleeing like rabbits with a dog after us, and I had the idea that the Ruud was running interference off to the right, closing the trap. The Walker was still some way behind us, and there was a lot of tree cover, but I was still thinking, *Why hasn't he crisped us?*

Was it the flies? Because the air was thick with them by then, and maybe they were screwing with the Walker's targeting. Or maybe the son of a bitch was just enjoying himself, the lordly Boyar out hunting peasants.

Sturgeon was in the lead, and without warning he disappeared, so completely that it was like a magic trick. More woodland real estate was going up in smoke, so any shout he gave was utterly lost. A moment later, Lawes was gone too, and then I was skidding to a halt at the edge of a big square hole, that had been covered over with branches and leaf litter before my comrades had crashed into it.

I imagined spikes. I imagined… well, to be honest my imagination was going nuts about then because I think I imagined crocodiles or something, but then Sturgeon was calling, telling us to get down there. With the Walker thundering closer, we didn't need much encouragement. Franken popped an incendiary in an adjacent tree as he brought up the rear, so that our exit would be just one more hotspot for the Walker to pass over.

CHAPTER FIVE

WHAT WE'D FOUND was a tunnel, too cramped to stand up in, which my HUD compass claimed ran north-east/south-west. We took the arm that led away from the water and put as much distance between us and the hole as we could. The crazy skimming of my gun's flashlight showed the tunnel was walled with concrete slabs, many of them defaced. My HUD translator kept picking up graffiti as we went, so that we made our escape through a cloud of overlaid Swedish obscenities.

I say, escape. That makes it sound happier than it was. What actually happened was that we came suddenly out into a big chamber lit by a couple of flickering electric lamps. The floor was some way below, and we stumbled and skidded down a rough flight of breezeblock stairs and into the muzzles of at least a dozen guns.

Sturgeon was already on hands and knees at the foot of the stairs – not shot, but the clumsy bastard had tripped over his own feet, his own gun skidding conveniently out of reach. Lawes was after him, aiming back at our new hosts, grimacing enough to show every one of his brown teeth.

There were at least fifteen of them there, men and women wearing a grab-bag of civvies and military cast-offs; armor vests and Barbour jackets and Vintersorg reunion tour T-shirts. Their guns – by far their most attention-grabbing feature given where they were pointed – were mostly surplus, assault rifles of the model before the model the current national army were toting, but there were a couple of ours there as well.

"I think we found the partisans," Cormoran said softly from behind me. "You want a flash-bang?"

She could blind them with her drones but I imagined the enclosed space with that many guns going off. If someone pulled a trigger right now, just about everyone was going to die from terminal ricochets.

"Easy now, let's not make this worse," I said, and saw that none of them understood me. They weren't Rurisksdottir's well-equipped lot; they didn't have translators, and they'd have to crowd inconveniently close to hear mine.

"Sarge?" Sturgeon asked. He had slowly tipped himself back until he was sitting on the bottom step.

"Go for it," I invited, and he tried something in Swedish that was good enough for my translator to recognize it.

There followed the expected give and take where they told us to put our guns down, and we politely declined.

At the same time I was making plain that we weren't there to shoot anyone, and that we were just a peaceful little search and rescue team. It was really, really hard to phrase all of this, partly because I didn't want to tax Sturgeon's vocabulary, and partly because we were Americans, and Americans were very definitely fighting the Nord army right about then, and so it was kind of hard to put the innocent face on.

They didn't seem to be buying it, and I was keenly aware of just how twitchy people get when this sort of stand-off goes on for any length of time. Then a new voice broke in, and a lot changed as soon as it did. It was a woman's high, light voice, and the partisans shuddered when she spoke. Moreover, she was speaking some jabber that didn't sound at all like Swedish, and that my translator gave up on from the get-go.

But Sturgeon answered her tentatively, fumbling for words. He was a smart guy for languages, Sturgeon. When the 203rd had been given its marching orders, he'd been cramming like there would be a test and everyone had laughed at him. How glad was I that he was a goddamn intellectual right then? Damn glad, I can tell you.

She stepped forward, and the partisans gave her plenty of room. That would have been the time to shoot them, I reckon, but I was too startled by what I was looking at.

She was as slight as Sturgeon, and shorter, and her hair was swept back wetly like it had been gelled. She didn't have a gun trained on us, although there was a long-barreled pistol-looking weapon stuck through her belt.

She had some sort of uniform on, pouches and clips and pockets but no rank or insignia. It ended at her elbows and knees, but I didn't see that at first, because the skin of her limbs was fuzzy with sleek hair. Her eyes were cat's eyes glinting in the electric light. Her feet were bare. I was being slow, right then; only the bare feet joined the dots for me. I remembered those footprints near where our man Jerome had been nabbed.

It was a fine time to discover my Californian translator didn't know Finnish.

She looked into our guns without any apparent fear, but I had a sense of a coiled spring in her, as if she could go faster than bullets.

"She wants to know why the Russian is after us," Sturgeon explained.

"You get the impression she and the Russian are best buds?" I asked him.

"Sarge, I don't know."

I looked at the woman and she looked back at me – she was real uncanny valley territory. She was beautiful – that's how they'd made her. She was beautiful and she wasn't human. She scared the bejesus out of me.

"Tell her we don't know, but he and his Ruudboys have been after us for a while."

"I thought these guys were on the same side as the Whites," Cormoran murmured, but I'd put my words into Sturgeon's mouth and he was saying them. I was playing to my gut, letting something inside me that was all instinct and no thought decode that near-kin body language of hers.

The Finn woman nodded sharply and said something to the partisans, which a couple of the more learned had to translate to the rest.

"She said we're all friends then," Sturgeon translated. "Although the rest don't seem to see it that way."

"Can't think why." I leant in close. "All right, you're always claiming you're such a smart guy, find a nice polite way of asking her why they're not shooting us dead."

The rest of us settled on the stairs, with our guns not quite pointed at the partisans, and the partisans settled at their end of the room with their guns not quite pointed at us. The Finn girl stood apart from them – and I watched them as their eyes tracked her, and at least one of them crossed himself when he thought she wasn't looking. When Sturgeon spoke to her, his hands were constantly in motion, gesturing and clutching to reach past the gaps in his Finnish. She stood absolutely still, a cat watching a mouse hole. Jesus, but she scared me.

Franken got out some ration bars, something to chew on while we had the chance. His robot brain had shut up – some time during the fight it had apparently suicided, perhaps clicking that we were using it as an early warning system.

I saw when Sturgeon got the big news – he almost jumped in the air with it, and then spent some painful minutes getting the woman to repeat whatever she'd said before hotfooting it over to us.

"What's the deal?" I was watching the partisans, who were looking more and more twitchy now that the Finn was talking to us.

"She knows we're after the Scion," Sturgeon got out.

"Fuck." Abruptly we were also tense as hell, which did nothing for the anxiety attack the locals were having. "And how? You let that slip?"

"No, Sarge. She saw him. She said she couldn't think who else we'd be out here after."

"Saw him –"

"She knows where they took him. Or her people do, anyway. I, er…" He grimaced. "From what she said, there's not much goes on around here they don't see."

I glanced at Cormoran. "Those flies of theirs, they spy stuff out?"

She looked uncertain for about the first time since we'd met. "I really want to say no, Sarge, but…" She shrugged.

"So…?" I prompted Sturgeon.

"She's ready to go. She's ready to take us."

"Why?" Franken broke in. "Why would she? Got to be a trap, Sarge."

"Yeah." I nodded, thoughtfully. The Finn woman was watching me – not us, but *me* – and I wondered if she could hear us, and if she could understand.

Sturgeon looked stubborn. "More of a trap than being stuck in a small room with a bunch of Nord irregulars, Sarge?"

"Yeah, I can think of lots worse traps than that – shit!" Because in that eyeblink between looking over at her and looking back at Sturgeon, she'd come up right close to us, close enough for me to jab her with my rifle barrel. She said something in her jabber – it was weird, that language, sounded half Nord and half music – and then she almost flowed up the stairs, aided by everyone's very strong desire not to be touched by her.

"She said to come on," Sturgeon said, and then, not that I'd asked, "Her name's Viina."

Everyone was waiting for my order, and what decided me was the thought that, with Bioweapon Viina out of the room, the forbearance of the partisans was unlikely to last very long. Swearing, I got to my feet and led the charge after her.

She took us past where we'd entered the tunnels, moving into the dark without a flashlight and letting us blunder after her. Cramped spaces and poor light make for a very tense Sergeant Ted Regan, and I swear I nearly shot her three times just from pure nerves. We broke out into the forest at last, to find that dusk had snuck up on us. I didn't reckon that Viina was one to just set up camp and wait for the morning, though, so we were all on night ops until further notice. I wondered if she needed to sleep at all, or whether half her brain napped at a time, like dolphins.

Cormoran was doing what she could with her drones; all she could tell me was that we were veering back toward the lake, but that we were probably going parallel to the vehicle tracks we'd found before the Walker and its mechs stumbled on us.

"So why's she helping, Sturgeon?" I pressed, punching him in the shoulder. "Or are we just trusting your magic girlfriend?"

He threw me a hurt look. "What I heard, the whole thing's

gone to crap on their side. The Walker's been hunting the partisans down, and they reckon they've been sold out by the government – or maybe just by the corporations. They say they're the only true patriots left in Sweden, that they don't trust anyone. They want to make their own state, basically, run the place themselves."

"And so nobody can control them." I was thinking ahead, because some time in the future everyone would be in a place where we could sign a piece of paper and agree just how much of Nordland could be picked clean by the corporations – ours and theirs – and if there were a load of armed natives still determined to be at war, well, that'd be real awkward for all concerned.

"Yeah, so they've been fighting just about everybody, except the Finns."

"Why not the Finns?"

"Because whatever the crap the Finns want, it's not Swedish land," Sturgeon explained.

"How about you give me your best guess as to what they do want."

"Sarge, I have not the first idea. Unless they don't want anything, and them being here is a test."

"A test of what? Of *them*?" Because Viina was a weapon, and weapons needed testing. "So why is Little Miss Loaded Gun there leading us to Cousin Jerome?"

"I think she's curious," Sturgeon told me. "I think she wants to know what he was doing here, too."

And that was when the White Walker, which had been sitting very quietly amongst the trees, running its systems cold as the night air, suddenly rammed everything up to high gear and turned its lights on. We were caught like rabbits in the headlamps as the night was split with a thunderous screaming sound.

The Russian was coming to get us, and he was playing some serious thrash metal from his suit's speakers. Everyone's a comedian.

We legged it through the trees, with the major disadvantage that we didn't have many trees left because Viina had brought us out closer to the water than before. Behind us, the Walker rose to its full height and took its first stomping step.

We tried to keep to the forest, but there were Ruuds out there too – spindly shapes suddenly flashing hot in our sight, the Russian's hunting dogs stilting along and herding us toward the open ground. Franken lit one up with a scatter of grenades and incendiaries and left it burning, but by then we were basically out of woods, and we were a *lot* closer to the water than I'd reckoned on.

I remember turning, on that strip of ravaged farmland we found ourselves on, with the great darkness of the Vättern at our backs. One of the Ruuds plowed out of the treeline with Cormoran's remotes circling and buzzing it like hawks. It fixed on us, minigun swinging, and then one of the drones rammed it right in its camera-lens face and exploded, rocking the thing back with its chassis suddenly torn open and on fire. And all of this in silent mime because the thunder and bass of the White Walker's music was the only thing our ears had room for.

When Sturgeon's voice came, though, it came in my earphone, cutting through the row. "Sir! She's –!"

He was already halfway to the water – I caught him gesturing, but the signs made no sense, and then the Walker came out of the trees and I had other priorities. I was about to get set on fire by some oligarch's favored son.

We shot at it; of course we shot at it. We peppered it with grenades and AP rounds and incendiaries and whatever little peashooter the remaining drone had. It stood there and let us, our shot lighting it up with constellations of doomed little impacts that did no damage at all.

The music went dead. The night seemed very, very quiet after that; my ears were buzzing with the silence. The White Walker actually leant toward us a little, as though choosing who it was going to kill first. Then one of its shoulder pods spoke, and a shell spiraled madly overhead before arcing back and plowing into the forest with a flare that left jittery after-images across my HUD. Another two followed – one soaring far off over the Vättern before extinguishing itself, and another seeming to go straight up, detonating like a firework and spattering the water's edge with shreds of burning phosphorus, sending us all running. Right then I still thought he was playing with us, until I glanced up. In the Walker's lights, the air danced and glittered and seethed

It wasn't just my ears that were buzzing. Over my head, the air was thick with flies. The flares and echo-shapes on my HUD were just the edge of the vast cloud of ECM interference that were sending the Walker's targeting haywire.

"Where's the Finn?" I yelled, because she was doing this somehow; she had to be.

"Bloody hell!" Lawes' voice, far too loud in my earpiece, and then the Brit was throwing himself aside from something. I saw the shadow of it with my eyes, but my HUD told me it wasn't there, just a piece of cool night sprinting toward the Walker on all fours.

It got to within ten feet of the Walker and leapt, finding a perch up there amongst all that obsolete heraldry. I glimpsed something humanoid but not human, long-limbed and ragged with hair. Then I saw another, springing up to the Walker's shoulders. There were more; they had come out of the water behind us, silent and sleek: Viina had not been operating alone.

We stood very still, we humans, save when the Walker stomped forward and we made room for it. This had suddenly become a fight in which human beings were entirely optional. It was a battle of competing technologies.

And still I wondered how the Finns could actually achieve anything. Let them be swift and strong as bears and tigers, it wouldn't mean jack against all that armor. The flies were still coming, though, swarming through the air to settle on the Walker's hull like we were watching some piece of film run in reverse. It was like the Scion was drawing them out of the air. They were coating his weapons, his vents, every part of him that promised access to the meat below.

My HUD began to tell me a story then. The White Walker was starting to live up to its name on the thermal imaging: from red to orange, growing hotter and hotter as the thickening carpet of engineered insects blocked its heat sinks. And all the while the Finns danced across its surface, prying and wrenching.

Its shoulder pod exploded. I caught a brief afterimage of a torn near-human shape being flung away, but then all the ammunition was going up, each shell setting off the next, and the whole area became a very unhealthy place to be. We continued our escape along the water's edge, leaving the battle to forces entirely beyond us in power and sophistication.

Sturgeon says... Well, hell, by the time I stopped running and turned around, it was mostly over. I saw the Walker on the ground and on fire, and then something fundamental went off and there were pieces of armor and favored son raining down all over.

Sturgeon says that a crab the size of a Buick came out of the Vättern and scissored one of the Walker's legs off at the knee, but I'm not falling for that. Even in this world of ours, such things just don't happen.

I did a head count; we'd all made it, bar the drone that had given its artificial life to take out the Ruud. For a moment I thought – *hoped* – that we'd seen the last of Viina and her compatriots. But no, here they came, a full dozen of them ghosting without warning from the shadow and the pitch. Two legs, but they didn't walk like us; human features but animal expressions. We had our guns up, all of us, and they didn't show any fear at all. I know that the movies lie. I know that if I've got my finger on the trigger and my sights on a target, there's no way they can rush me before I punch a hole in them. That's been a point of faith for me all my professional life. Facing the dogs, then, I lost that faith. They came from the darkness like wolves from old stories, the killers that taught us to fear the night. When Viina grinned, I saw fangs. They looked at us with the arrogance of top predators. The arrogance of youth, too: how old could they have been, how quickly had they been force-grown in their labs? Or were there breeding populations of these things over the border? Had they already broken away from their creators?

Sturgeon says it was going for decades before the war: the US was tightening up on whole areas of science that the Christ Lib crowd and the other fundamentalists were crying blasphemy on. A lot of Europe was going the same way for secular or religious reasons, and there had been that outbreak in China that had suddenly made them way less keen on biosciences as the future of military superiority. The funding dried up and the laws came in, and a great many scientists just found a different area to work in, preferably for one of the agriscience multinationals, because that was where the money was.

Except there were some researchers who didn't care about breeding a new strain of wheat that would outperform its competitors and then conveniently die off so you had to buy more. There were some who had been playing with the blasphemy label since before the Christ Lib people got hold of it. Those men and women who were long on genius and short on ethics needed somewhere to go.

I have no idea what was going on in Finnish politics or

academia which led to that place becoming a covert haven for mad scientists. Sure as hell it wasn't the only one, but they were maybe the most subtle. Five years before I signed up there was what the media called Operation Frankenstein in Bolivia, when the boffins over there got a bit too open about what they were making. There was never an Operation Moreau kicking in doors in Helsinki, though, and we were face to face with the results of that oversight.

"So, what now?" I asked. I was going for defiant, but Sturgeon's shaky translation sounded pitiful.

One of the males muttered something that sounded hungry, and a couple of them laughed, cruel and malevolent as hyenas. Then Viina spoke, in that voice that sounded almost like singing. Her eyes glowed in the moonlight.

"She says, let's find your..." Sturgeon grimaced. "*Perillinen*. Which is probably Scion." He paused, listened to the next words. "She says she'll show us. She says it's not even far."

"Where are they off to?" Lawes hissed. Even as Sturgeon had been speaking, some of the Finns had just walked off into the water, as if it was the most natural thing in the world. One by one they dived and were lost in the cold lake, hidden behind the moon's reflection, and I thought, *Not wolves; otters.*

"She says..." Sturgeon was listening intently. "She says that she has... ah, *siunaaminen* something... She's..."

Viina walked forward, slipping between our guns, cutting between me and Sturgeon, close enough to brush us both with her fingers before we jumped aside. She was going for Cormoran, who backed off hurriedly as the Finn reached out a hand.

"No, it's your drone, she says she's – blessed? – your drone. She... Again please?"

Viina looked back at him with amusement and made fluttering motions with her hands.

Sturgeon nodded hurriedly. "Your drone can fly now. Your drone can follow the track. You'll see. Follow her, but send the drone ahead."

I nodded permission, and Cormoran sent her last remaining remote ahead. Viina said one word, and it was obviously, "Follow," or something close.

"What about the rest of them?" Franken demanded. "Why aren't they coming?"

What Viina had to say about that, after Sturgeon translated, well... She said there were a lot of men where we were going. Did we really want all of them dead?

CHAPTER SIX

However she did it, Viina blessed that drone good. Cormoran flew it through that fly-spattered air and never lost signal once.

The trail took us inland at the start like Cormoran had said, then it broke out of the trees and shadowed the course of a road that the fighting had left shattered like a long strip of jigsaw pieces. All this time we were following on foot, while Cormoran had one eye on the terrain in front of her and one on the drone's camera feed. We'd reached the road ourselves when she called a halt. "All right, this you've got to see."

What it was, was a castle. This was Europe, and suddenly it had become the Europe we Americans were always promised, because the bad guys were holed up inside an honest-to-God ruined castle. And in the bombed-out restaurant and parking lot across the road from it, but that doesn't sound half as impressive.

My HUD map called it *Brahehus* and it was obvious that the end had come for it a long time before anyone thought of airstrikes. It had a few intact walls, though, and the drone showed that there was a prefab cabin pitched in there, and a bigger camp outside the walls around a space that had been cleared and flattened as a landing pad. This wasn't just some temporary camp. There were plenty of men there; a handful of vehicles. They had been there a while.

"Come on," I said, and Viina was pacing back and forth like she was about to just take off without us. Cormoran was still messing with the images, though, panning and searching until at last she said, "There!"

They'd roofed off the castle with heat baffles, but the drone had snuck in under them, neat as you like, creeping into that covered space through the gaping eyesocket space where a window had once been. It took a single image before retreating, and even then the enemy security grid had started to wonder if something was wrong. Cormoran did a lot of finagling to stay undetected that long.

We got a good look at that single image of the cabin, as Cormoran zoomed and let her software's pattern recognizers do their work.

There was a shape through the window there. We couldn't exactly buzz the drone down to head level to be certain, but it sure as hell looked like an American-made Scion shell to me. We'd found our man. Or we'd found his metal clothes, but either way it was the best lead in a field of one.

*   *   *

IT TOOK US a day's walk to catch up with the drone, keeping under cover wherever we could and hoping that nobody else's remote eyes had been 'blessed' by the Finns. Viina kept going in and out – now loping alongside us, then just gone for an hour or more on her own business. She made it painfully clear that we were slowing her down. She looked at us as though we were... Jesus, I don't know: pets; barely tolerated cripples; last year's models.

We let the dark gather before we got too close to the castle. I mean, sure, we'd all show up on thermals – except Viina – but no sense in making things easy for them.

By that time, Cormoran had built up a picture of how security worked there and got a few clues as to who these clowns were.

"Corporate," she told us. "Not Skaalmed, and their insignia isn't flagging up as known, but their gear is good. If they were just sitting tight, I think we'd be screwed, but they're packing up."

Lawes was staring close at her screens, eyes narrowed. "'Cos the front's moving this way," he suggested. "They want to scram before our side get here."

"They're moving our man out then?" Franken put in, "Reckon we can grab him on the road?"

"They'll be traveling faster than we can, now we've lost the Trojan," I pointed out. "We're not equipped to strike a convoy."

Lawes looked up at me. "You're going to suggest we walk in there, aren't you."

"They're not friends of yours, then? I thought you knew all the Nord corporate types."

"Even the ones I know, they wouldn't exactly want me walking in on some Scion-kidnapping operation."

He wasn't quite looking me in the eyes, which I guess was normal for him, but my gut said to press him. "Who are they, Lawes?"

He bared his teeth again, that tic of his that made him look like he was trying to use bad dentistry like a threat display. "There, that badge there. That's the field operations division of LMK. The big agri boys: Lantgård Mass Kemisk."

"They're on our side, aren't they?" Franken asked slowly.

"No, no they're not," Lawes told him. "I mean, yes, there's a US subsidiary, just like there's a Nord one and an Indian one and, you know, anywhere there's money. They're one of the big players here, though."

"They asked us in," Cormoran recalled. "Or they were one of the corps requesting US help when the Nord govs turned socialist."

"And they've been pitching into the fight ever since, whenever it looked like the US corp forces were getting too much of an upper hand." Lawes glowered at the lot of us, then jabbed a finger at Sturgeon. "Ask him, he knows. If you think this is a fight between US and Nord govs then you're bloody morons. This is corps versus corps using poor bastards like us as the meat in the grinder."

"Because it's cheaper for them to have the army die in their place," Sturgeon agreed softly.

"Enough of that," I snapped. "What this *is*, is a rescue operation. Those are our orders. Let Capitol Hill and Stockholm sort out the big picture between them. We're going to go in, grab our man and get out."

Lawes stared at me. Well, they all stared at me, but I remember Lawes most.

"You're cracked," he spat out. "Sarge, sod me but you're mad. LSK are serious business from South Africa to the sodding Arctic Circle. We do *not* want to go poke them with a stick."

"No, soldier, I don't *want* to, but it looks like they're leaving me no choice," I told him.

"It's suicide."

"No, it's just us doing our jobs."

"It's suicide, just to go drag out some over-privileged nancy boy who's stupid enough to get himself caught. You think they won't just ransom him back when they're done? You think anybody's going to ransom us?"

"That's our mission," I told them.

"They've got a couple hundred men in there," Lawes snapped. "They've got better gear than us."

"And most of them aren't at that castle, they're over the road in the main camp," I pointed out patiently. "I reckon whoever's in charge just couldn't resist pitching his command in an actual castle, and so he's ended up separate to most of his force. Now, I'm not suggesting we take the place by storm. We're going to exploit their officer's dumbass ideas about living history and do this sneaky. I thought sneaky was what you did, Lawes."

"You think LSK have such toss security that I can walk straight in? We're not exactly corporate industrial espionage over here."

"Well, actually," said Cormoran, which diverted all that aggrieved disbelief from me. She shrugged. "The ECM from the fly-screen is screwing with their systems a lot. Now it's not touching mine, I can start messing with them."

"Can you cut us a gap in the fence?" I was thinking about thermal and motion sensors and just plain cameras, the sort of security even a mobile base like this would have.

She was looking at the screens of her case again. "Their systems are shielded against casual intrusion," she said, eyes narrowed. "Gonna need to go hammer some spikes in. That means someone getting there on foot and not tripping the alarm." She looked up at us brightly. "And it's not going to be me. It'll take all my concentration to open a gap, and twice that to keep it open."

"So once we've got a gap?"

She grinned, a brief flash of white teeth. "Then your handpicked elite go and see if our man's still there. Take the drone with you and get it close to their data systems. They're not open to access from outside queries, but with a bit of proximity you never know. I'll see what I can read while you're over there."

"Because you won't be one of my elite, right?"

"Sure as hell no." Unapologetic as you please.

"Fine then: spike their defenses; team go in; spring our

guy; GTFO." Perhaps not one of my most sophisticated plans.

"Who gets to go spike?" Sturgeon asked. Nobody was falling over themselves to volunteer. Cormoran's spikes were little data relays someone would have to splice into the corps system. Once in, they would act as open terminals for her signals, letting her turn whole sections of their grid on and off, hopefully without being noticed.

My eyes had turned to Lawes. I'd seen the tech he was carting about with him. He squinted back at the drone image, obviously turning the odds over in his mind. "Your Mr bloody Speling better be good for the bonus," he muttered grudgingly

He upended his pack and brought out his sneak-suit, which would mask his heat signature – and fry him if he wore it for too long. It was patterned with slow-shifting shadows that broke up his silhouette and muddied his movements, all the cues that electronic or human security would be attuned to. With his skinny frame got up in that, his face hidden by goggles and a bandit-style bandana, it was hard to focus on him even standing there in front of us. There would be electronics in the cloth to screw with motion sensors, too, and even then he would have to be damn careful.

We went over the details again, the signal, the timing – he had thirty minutes to get somewhere before he'd need to pull out, or we'd assume that he'd been compromised. It was a pain in the ass that we couldn't send a drone in with him, but Cormoran would be busy redirecting their systems, and she didn't have a second drone to spare any more. Besides, if the enemy's security was any good, then they'd be keyed up to detect drone infiltration rather than human. After all, why would they expect that anyone would be stupid enough to just walk into their base?

We lost track of Lawes once he'd left us, which meant he was doing something right. Cormoran was working, and the rest of us got to just sit around. I'd already decided that I'd go in myself, if Lawes could cut us a big enough hole, and I'd take Franken with me because if Cousin Jerome really was there, and not able to just walk on his own feet, we'd need someone big to carry him. Sturgeon and Cormoran would be our cover, if we came out hot.

I'd half expected Viina to volunteer her services when it came to going in, but she was just sitting back with her knees gathered up to her chin and watching us with that cool, alien amusement. If she actually understood what we were about, there was no indication of it.

Just short of twenty minutes into our time and Cormoran said, "He's doing it. I'm getting access. First spike is online. Yeah, that's good." Headware feeding her the data, she nodded blindly at her own mind's eye. "I'm in. No alarms tripped. I see the security grid... trying to isolate the cabin from the main camp." Abruptly she grimaced. "No, no..." Her hands twitched, old keyboard reflexes surfacing briefly. "No, got it. Come on Lawes, don't make me cover for you. It thinks it's seen him... rerouting queries... The security's... well, it's OK, I guess. Always the problem with field ops like theirs, you never quite get the..." She went on, little scraps of sentences, half to us, half talking to a Lawes whose existence and actions she was having to infer from what she saw going on in the LMK system, and who couldn't hear her in any event. And then at last, "Yeah, we're good, we're good. That looks stable, at least until they do a sweep... and there's the signal. Over to you, Sergeant." My HUD sprang up with a ground overlay showing me the corridor she'd cut through their security.

I nodded to her and to Sturgeon, with one last glance at Viina in case she had decided we required her services. She hadn't moved: apparently we were doing the next bit monster-free.

We got half the way there before Lawes popped up in front of us, almost in arm's reach before we saw him. A moment later he was desperately stripping away the camouflage. Inside, he was the color of well-done lobster.

"Christ, I hate those bloody things," he hissed, and just stared down Franken when the man growled at him. "Fuck me, don't make me do that again."

"Stop complaining and let's move before all your hard work gets overwritten," I told him.

The three of us followed Cormoran's invisible road, briefly skirting the edge of the main camp before heading up to the castle. I could already see that Bahehus hadn't exactly been Fort Knox even back in the day. The windows weren't little slits that a man could get arrow-shot through, but were great big open holes in the walls – enough that it seemed more hole than wall in parts. Most of these had been screened over, but the whole place was still little more than period decoration for whatever was inside. They were relying on their system spotting any intruder, which was their bad luck.

Lawes pulled us down, and we watched a trio of men pass along the foot of the castle wall before heading toward the main camp. They didn't seem overly alert, and they were talking amongst themselves – my translator didn't catch more than a few words, but I recognised the tone. These were soldiers at the end of their duty, eager to get back to their buddies. In the army, we said that corp forces had the best gear and the best pay, but they knew fuck all about proper discipline half the time. Apparently it was no different amongst the Nords.

Then we were creeping further in, right up to the wall, and I'll bet Franken was praying to Christ Lib that Cormoran had done her job properly or this was going to break all known records for going FUBAR. No klaxons and no red lights, though; more to the point no bullets coming our way.

There was a front way into the castle courtyard where the cabin was, but none of us felt quite that confident. Instead, Lawes took one of the screened windows, isolated a trip-switch that would have started yelling, and then cut a slit in the plastic. He sized up Franken, widened the slit a bit, then made 'after you' gestures.

"We'll need more than that," I murmured. "We might be coming out of here with a body."

For a moment Lawes stared at me blankly, but then he nodded and turned the slit into a flap, securing it with a clip to stop it flapping once we'd all clambered through.

There were lights on in the cabin, and I did wonder whether we'd end up bagging some LMK director as a hostage. If our guy wasn't there, and Cormoran couldn't trawl it from their system, then we'd need someone to point us in the right direction, after all.

It's amazing how far ahead of yourself you can get, if you're not keeping your mind on the here-and-now.

So we crept up to that cabin. The front was all lit up, but the side where we were was shadowy, and still within the footprint of Cormoran's attentions.

Lawes signaled: did I want to try the front door? I didn't, because no amount of electronic wizardry would keep us from just physically being seen.

"I'll go round the back," he said, just a whisper in my helmet receiver. "Hold here."

When he was gone, I took the chance to examine the cabling running from the cabin. Most of it was clamped to the wall with staples, and some of it would be power, but maybe some was data. I got Cormoran's drone out and moved it from one to another until it gave me a green light, like she'd said it would. Clamped there, it would try to read the LMK dataflow, and maybe it would turn up something useful if we found nothing more than an empty shell inside.

"Come round the back, Sarge, I've got it sorted," buzzed Lawes in my ear, and so we did, and we found Lawes there with a good dozen LMK soldiers, all waiting quiet as you please with their guns on us. We didn't even get the chance to return the favor like we did with the partisans.

Franken growled, deep in his chest, and I put a hand on his shoulder. Inside, I felt exactly the same, and when Lawes grinned at us I wanted to shove every one of those big teeth down his throat.

"When?" I asked him flatly.

He spread his hands. "Look, you're new in this neck of the woods, right? You think you know how it works, us, them, all that shit. Only I told you it ain't like that. Friends today are enemies tomorrow and the other way round. I've been here since the start. I've made bloody sure I kept on the good side of the big players, whichever side they were playing. You think I want to be on LMK's shit list? You think I want to get myself killed on some bloody stupid suicide mission just because some rich Yank moron's got himself caught?"

"It wasn't a suicide mission," I ground out between my teeth.

"Not until you sold us out, you little shit," Franken added, with considerable restraint. "How the fuck did you even have time?"

The Nord officer there laughed at that. "Oh, your friend here came right to us," he explained in almost accentless English. "He was telling us his whole story while my men were splicing in your spikes. He wanted us to just send men to secure your team, but that sounded too much like a trap to me. Now we have you, we'll go pick up your friends. Hopefully they won't resist."

I said nothing. There didn't seem to be much point lying about our numbers or capabilities, not when Lawes was being so obliging for them.

They took our guns, disarmed us smartly of anything more dangerous than a spoon. I'd lost comms on the instant, all channels cut. I couldn't send a warning to Sturgeon and Cormoran, but I hoped to hell that they'd notice I was suddenly off the grid.

The LMK officer cocked his head. "Do you want to see your target, Sergeant Regan, isn't it?" He must have taken my sullen grunt for confirmation, because he had the pair of us taken round the front of the cabin and escorted into the front door. The place looked like every prefab admin hut I ever saw: desk, terminal, furniture, and a couple of bunks at the back. There was paper, too, because nobody out in the field ever relies 100% on the electronics. Every soldier knows that things always go wrong. Of course, for us they'd gone wrong all at once and without warning.

The Scion was there, too. It was seated, although the legs must have been taking a lot of the weight because the metal frame chair didn't look that sturdy. The shine of its chassis had taken more than a few knocks – it needed a polish before it was fit for the parade ground, certainly. The sculpted face, between and above its broad shoulderplates, was a good enough approximation of Cousin Jerome's to give me positive ID.

Our captor rapped sharply on its chest. In truth the armor was too thick for it to sound hollow, but I got the point. Our man was long gone to some Nord gulag or interrogation suite. Not exactly a huge surprise – my dreams of finding Jerome in the flesh and spiriting him away had always been mostly wishful thinking – but right then the Nord banging on his shell sounded like someone hammering nails into my coffin.

"So where is he?" Maybe I thought it was one of those movie moments, where the bad guys explain all their plans. If so, the Nord officer hadn't seen that kind of movie.

"I don't believe that's information you require, Sergeant."

"What happens to us?"

His smile wasn't unpleasant, in its own way. "Sent for debrief. Prisoners of war. What's the line? For you, the war is over."

I nodded, impassive, almost as if I hadn't heard him. Mostly this was because something had flashed on my HUD. It was showing me a handful of status bars: my biosigns and other data it could get from me. Everything else was blocked, though, in or out. Except something had flashed in the corner of the corner of my eye just then, a rapid sequence of characters.

Franken grunted. To anyone else it would have sounded like nothing so much as brute resentment about our position. To me, who'd known him for so long, it told me he'd had the same.

"We'd ship you out by air," the LMK officer was saying as his men ushered us out of the prefab, "but you wouldn't thank me for it. That damned muck the Finns let out into the air gets into the engines. So it'll be by road, but it won't be so bad."

And I was nodding along, but the signal came and came again. The characters blurred past very fast. 'I' was first, G last. Was it a code? Was it just a word?

We were clearing the castle walls, crossing toward the road, toward the main camp. I was concentrating so hard I tripped and almost faceplanted the path.

I-N-?????-N-G

The officer had asked me a question. I tried to reconstruct it, but I'd missed it entirely.

Franken came to my rescue. "He's just tired. We've been on the move for weeks." So the officer probably thought I was drunk, and I couldn't blame him.

"Give me a moment." Shaking my head as if to clear it.

"Get him up," the officer directed, and I was hauled to my feet. I could see he was suspicious as hell. "What's wrong with him."

It came again. I saw it – I must have been really obvious because he grabbed my helmet and yanked it, twisted it off my head and nearly cut my throat with the chinstrap doing so. It didn't matter. I'd seen the signal. I'd seen what it said.

Incoming.

Cormoran had got in. They were coming to rescue us.

This failed to fill me with cheer, because it sounded like the best possible way to get the rest of my squad captured or killed.

The officer had a pistol out and he jammed it under my chin while his men held me. "*Vad* är *du gör?*" he snarled, too angry for English and of course the translator was in my helmet. I could play dumb with real conviction.

Then he was gone. It was so sudden I thought he'd shot me. I could still feel the steel finger of the pistol at my throat even though it had been torn away. Then the killing started.

I saw the officer lying dead at my feet with his head mostly ripped from the rest of him. One of his men was twisting my arm behind my back – as if I could have had anything to do with it. The other had let go, was bringing his gun up. I heard shouting in Swedish.

I saw Viina. Just for a moment in the darkness, I saw her. She slammed into the LMK soldiers and cut two of them open, body armor and all, then turned and loosed a spray of bullets from her long-barrelled gun. Franken was free, grabbing up a rifle from the ground. I rammed my head back into the face of the man that had me, glancing painfully off his chin. It was enough to loosen his grip and I tumbled forward out of it.

My helmet was there on the ground in front of me. I could see the HUD lighting up like Christmas.

Franken was down on one knee at my side, crouched low and not lifting the gun, because right now he wasn't anyone's target and he wanted to keep it that way. "Got an escape plan," he snapped out, eyes on his own display.

"Lead," I told him, snagged my helmet, and then we were both running. We were both running *back* toward the main camp. "Wait, this can't be right!" I hollered at Franken but he didn't hear. A moment later I had my own helmet on, wrestling with the strap, seeing the path overlaid in front of me – right into the heart of the enemy.

Franken turned, let me get past him and then opened up full auto back toward the castle, not trying to kill people so much as trying to make them keep their heads down. There was all sorts of commotion in the camp, of that you can be sure.

They had Ruuds. One of them leapt up from its collapsed-stick resting pose right ahead of us, its minigun already whining. The camp lights gleamed – no, they swirled, the air dancing about them like smoke. Then I was stumbling, waiting for the gunfire. I saw soldiers ahead of me, some of them in full battledress, most of them not. They looked as terrified and confused as I felt.

The Ruud shuddered and something screamed inside its body. It did a mad jig on its three stilting legs and then just starting shooting and loosing off shells – at random? No: there was one place it wasn't shooting and that was at me and Franken.

Men were running, falling, shouting, shooting back. The Ruud rocked with a dozen impacts, but the fit was on it like it was possessed. Around its body the flies danced like stars in the searing light, blocking any attempt by the LMK techs to reassert control.

Still, there was just one of it, and plenty of them. Abruptly bullets were tearing up the ground at my feet, and me without so much as a pea shooter. Franken returned fire, which is to say he was pissing into the hurricane. I didn't even know where we were running to.

Then I did. One of the enemy vehicles was suddenly outlined in blue, the universal color of the good guys. It was starting to move out, jerky at first but then rolling forward, an armored scout car that could have left our Trojan in the dirt.

I went for it, but then threw myself aside as the suppressive fire came in. One shot struck my body armor at an angle, not enough to floor me but enough to remind me how many parts of my body didn't have the benefit. The Ruud lurched into them then, spraying shot madly, dancing like a marionette. Some of the camp was on fire from the incendiaries. Another Ruud was active, but just standing and sparking.

Viina came past us like the north wind, now on two legs, now all fours. I saw her snatch up a dropped rifle and roll, emptying it at the enemy as she came up to her knees, and then she was running – she seemed almost fast enough to overtake her own bullets. When she struck the knot of LMK men I lost sight of her. I could only track her by the bodies she left behind.

Then I bounced off the side of the armored car, and the string of text on my HUD was saying *GETINGETINGETIN.*

"Viina!" I yelled. No human could have heard me, but who knew how good her ears were?

She broke from them – again, it was only by the reactions of the enemy I could tell. She was coming, dancing through the firefight, even as Franken tried to cover her.

The possessed Ruud exploded, and then the other one, the one that had just stood there, scything shards of metal every which way. One of them spanged off the vehicle over my head, and when I'd got through ducking, Viina was down. Shot? Caught by the blast? I couldn't say, but I was running already, pelting into the killing ground because somehow, in my head, she'd become one of *my* people, and I was damned if I was leaving her behind.

I was almost at her when someone shot me high in the

chest. I went down, feeling the colossal impact through my vest, like the punch of a giant. I was ten feet short of Viina, who was twisting, flapping, clawing at the ground towards me. She couldn't help me. I couldn't help me. I could barely breathe.

Then a knee came down on my chest, right where the shot had gone, and I screamed. It was Lawes, the little fucker. He had a pistol pretty much up my nose and his eyes were wide and mad. Probably he was saying something clever and English. He could have been quoting Shakespeare for all I heard him, even though he was crouching real low to deny Franken a shot.

I was willing Viina to get up and do something, but she'd been shot bad, far worse than me, though that balance was about to be redressed. If Lawes had just pulled the trigger I'd not be telling this, but I had so thoroughly screwed his plans that he had to tell me, had to explain just how much he hated me.

Then something flashed between us and basically rammed him in the face. I recognized Cormoran's drone in the moment before it drew back, the sheer fact of it dragging Lawes' gun barrel up to follow it.

I threw him off me. I had my breath back by then and he was a little guy. He staggered, tried to get me in his sights again, and then someone shot him through the groin. It might have been Franken; it might have been one of the Swedes – they weren't to know he was on their side, after all. Like Lawes always said, it was a complicated war.

I gathered up Viina, hugging her to my chest – she seemed

to weigh ridiculously little, like a child or a doll. She was bleeding badly, shaking, thrashing feebly. I was hurting her more just by trying to save her. I should have left her. She wasn't even human, after all. Would I have done it for a dog? A cat?

I did it for her. I lurched and staggered and gasped my way back to the vehicle, even as the camp went mad behind me. Cormoran had coopted another Ruud and it was driving the LMK boys back, just as mad and spasmodic as the first one. I saw her drone zip like a mad wasp through the open hatch ahead of me, while Franken blew all the ammo he had to try and cover me.

Then I was dumping Viina inside and clambering in after her. In the car, Sturgeon was at the wheel and Cormoran was sitting calmly at her open briefcase like she was doing nothing more taxing than updating her relationship status.

I turned, yelling for him, and Franken came in backward through the hatch. His armor vest was all ripped up and he had lost the gun. For a moment I was telling myself it was Viina's blood on him, but it was his; it was his own.

I dragged his trailing leg in and got the hatch closed, feeling the impact of more bullets against it. Sturgeon was moving out, looking back at all the mess we'd made when he should have been looking where he was going. Cormoran scrabbled for a medical kit.

Franken was clenched, every muscle pulling against the rest. He met my eyes, teeth gritted and his face twisted so much by the pain that I wouldn't have known him. I could hear Sturgeon's panicky swearing, and I gripped Franken's hand and told him to hang in there, even as Cormoran slapped painkiller tabs on the inside of his wrists and on his neck.

And Sturgeon just drove. At first he took the road, because it was simply the best way to put distance between us and the LMK base. After that he went back into the woods, guiding the Nord vehicle between the trees until we were surely past the point where Cousin Jerome had been snatched, past where we'd fought the White Walker or met the buried partisans.

I had to hope that the fly-screen above us would screw any attempts to track us, because otherwise distance just wouldn't be enough.

CHAPTER SEVEN

At last we stopped. Franken was under, and we'd patched him as best we could, but he'd lost a lot of blood and we hadn't exactly stolen a field hospital. I'd seen him shot before, but I'd never seen him so pale, like his own ghost. The moment we came to rest, Sturgeon was bolting back out of the pilot's seat to look at him, his hands wringing at each other.

"Stupid bastard," he muttered. "What was he thinking?"

Viina, we hadn't given meds to. She was still with us, just about, gut-shot and trembling, curled about her wound and keening at a pitch that was only just inaudible, like electronics feedback. When we went close she snarled and spat, but it was weak. We could have forced some tabs onto her, but Cormoran was against it. We didn't know what they'd do to her. They'd been made for humans, after all.

"Your drone good to go?" I asked her, looking up from Franken's corpse-like form. When she nodded, I told her to get it out and scouting. If LMK were on our trail, we needed to know. If we'd got ourselves on anyone else's radar, we needed to know.

"What now, Sarge?" Sturgeon asked in a whisper. "What do we do now?"

Fuck knows. I just shook my head. We were down two and out of leads. Time to head home and admit defeat, surely. Even my stubbornness has limits.

Except heading home would rely on the world leaving us alone, and it didn't sound as though we'd be granted that indulgence. Cormoran's sudden intake of breath brought me straight over to her screens.

"What?" I couldn't see anything there, no thermal, no visual, nothing. She was frantically adjusting parameters, swinging the drone in wide circles, casting for the scent.

For a moment, no more than a second, we saw them on her screens, loping grey through the night toward us. Then they were gone like specters.

"The Finns." My throat was abruptly dry.

"They've come for her," Cormoran confirmed.

"How can they even know?" I demanded. This whole war front was a fog of misdirection and interference, except for them. They just cut through it all and they didn't even carry radios.

"I think..." Sturgeon was still crouching over Franken. "I

read about some stuff – what our people think the Finns were working on, what, ten, fifteen years back? Before Operation Frankenstein went down in Bolivia and all the rest of the biolab havens stopped taking visitors. Comms through quantum entanglement, they said."

"Bullshit," I replied promptly.

"Speculation," was his mild correction. "But what they said was, nobody had got it to work, not in a man-made system, but some guy at Harvard reckoned biological systems would be better at it. Only that was about when all the funding got yanked and the Congressional Science Committee basically said it was all the work of the Devil. So we never found out. But maybe the Finns did."

"I second bullshit," Cormoran put in. "So how are we playing this? They coming to kick our asses for letting their warrior princess get killed, you reckon?"

I thought about how the White Walker had been taken down. This tinpot little Nord scout car was a cardboard box by comparison, and I had the distinct feeling we wouldn't be able to outrun them either.

"Nobody point a gun. Keep the hatch open. We come in peace, right?"

The other two nodded unhappily. Out past the hatch the night contained a thousand ghosts. Every moon-shadow, every moving branch was a Finnish werewolf.

I glanced at Cormoran. "By the way, that was good work with the Ruuds back there. I didn't realize you could even hack them that way."

She smiled slightly. "Normally? No. But I was in their

system, thanks to you, and one of their techs had left the codes lying around. Strong as the weakest link, right?" She shook her head. "Even then they're no pushovers. If it hadn't been for the fly-screen blocking the LMK from getting back in, I'd never have done it. You saw that, right?"

"I did."

"I wonder if you've had a chance to think about it, because that was just something that happened, to back me up. Because it's real easy to think of these Finn creations as if they're animals, something less than human, but they saw what I was doing instantly, long before the LMK techs cottoned on." Her eyes were haunted in the vehicle lights. "They're smart. Computer smart, human smart, who knows? Maybe smart like nothing anyone saw before."

She stopped speaking then. They'd arrived.

They slunk out of the darkness: solemn, slender, alien. Some had human eyes, and some had cats', and some the dark, featureless orbs of deer.

One of them put out a hand with claw nails, misted with wiry grey hair. The words he spoke were foreign, but I got the gist without needing a translation. *Give her to us.*

"She's all yours. She's right here, you come and take her." Slipping outside the car, giving him space to get in, it was a hard thing to do.

Two of them bore her out and laid her on the cold, root-ribbed ground, and then another was bending over her, slipping things from pockets in his fatigues. I wouldn't have been surprised to see fetishes and voodoo dolls, but they were pipettes and vials, some modern alchemy, dashed on her skin, jabbed into her veins, dropped into her forced-open mouth.

While that was going on, one of them came back to us, one of the females. She was tall, stoop-shouldered; her eyes were huge, an owl's merciless orbs, and I swear I saw the black darts of horns jutting from her fringe of tawny hair. She came and stared at Franken, and I'd seen people less dispassionate looking at road kill. But then that hunter's face wasn't made for expression. Maybe I'm doing her a disservice.

"It's not just you, you see," I told her. "It's us. We suffer too. We've got losses too." I didn't care whether she could understand me. I didn't know if Franken was still breathing.

She said something. The words were lost, but the rhythms of her speech, a little like Swedish, a little like some language spoken by prehuman elves of a thousand years ago, they washed over me. But she sounded sad. She sounded sympathetic. The bioengineered killing machine could spare a moment to come down to our level, to taste the grief of yesterday's men.

And then she was asking me a question, and I stared into that face and could not guess what. Sturgeon got it, though. He twitched and his eyes went wide.

"She says – Sarge, she says, she says they will save him – will try to save him, Sarge!"

I looked into those predator's eyes. There was nothing written there that I could read. "Save him how?"

"I don't know, sir, but – it's yes, right? Come on, Sarge, he's almost..." Sturgeon's voice shook. I guess he was a better friend than me, in the end.

What would Franken say? "Can we... can we wake him, ask him?" But I knew the answer. He was clinging to life with such a failing grip that to tug on that rope would be to send him falling away into the abyss. So what would he say, Franken the church-goer, the devout Christ Libber? Would he want to live, even though deliverance came from the paws of demons? Questions I couldn't answer for him. I could only answer for me. Did I let one of my squad die? Did I let my friend die? Or did I make him live, and damn his principles.

I'm selfish, in the end. Most of us are.

I nodded to the Finn, and Sturgeon retreated to the driver's seat as she started her work.

THEN IT WAS time for sleep, for whatever the Finns were doing wasn't quick. It wasn't any field surgery I recognised: no incisions, no blood, no struggle. Instead they hunched over their patients, with their potions and their elixirs. They were not mending by brute mechanical force. They were growing, changing, tending the bodies of their charges like gardeners.

Sturgeon took first watch, at his insistence. When he woke me for my shift, Cormoran was up as well, watching feedback from her drone as it flew just below the fly-screen and mapped out the country around us. I told her she should sleep; she said she'd slept. Her headware kept her going on just a couple of hours, she told me.

"I'll bet that cost more than all the gear I ever got from the army."

"Probably. Nothing but the best, right?" She shrugged. "You've got a plan, Sergeant? When we're done with feeding time at the zoo, what are your orders?"

"You think we should go back?"

"You're worried what people might think?" Said with a sidelong look and an arched eyebrow. When I nodded, her expression turned pitying. "Sergeant, what they'll think is, 'Holy fuck, they're not dead!'"

"What's that supposed to mean."

"Why do you think they sent you and yours on this little jaunt, Sergeant?"

"Because we get things done."

"Oho, that's it, is it? And you get things done, what, better than a crack corporate extraction team, do you?"

I opened my mouth to say, *We're not doing so bad*, except I was surrounded by manifest evidence to the contrary.

Cormoran snorted. "Seriously, one of their own goes missing, and what happens? They send three grunts nobody'll miss out of the 203rd and a treacherous little shit like Lawes. That sound to you that they actually even think Jerome Speling's still alive out there? That he *can* be rescued?"

"But there's you," I told her hotly. "You with your million-dollar skull candy and your million-dollar education. They sent you. So maybe the rest of us are just here to get you where you need to go and then bleed out on the ground while you do it."

"That's what you think, huh?"

"Damn straight."

"Well then let me tell you why I'm here, Sergeant Regan. I'm here because when my commanding officer thought he'd slum it and sleep with the help, I told him where he could get off. And I went on saying no right after he said he wouldn't take no for an answer." She was speaking quietly but her voice abruptly had an edge on it like broken glass. "And when he tried to put me over his desk I hacked his fucking phone and overclocked the battery so much they needed a surgeon to unmelt it from his thigh. So no, Sergeant, I am not here to perform a dance of corporate superiority over your cooling corpses. I am here to die like a dog, just as you are. So what are your orders?"

I remember how much hope just fell from me, right then. I hadn't realized that, however much I expected her to cast us off, I was still taking a lot of strength from the idea that *someone* on the team would accomplish the objective. An objective. Any objective. I'd imagined her suddenly calling down an unmarked corporate gunship to load Jerome onto, when we'd found him. And even if it flew off without me and mine – as it surely would have – at least the mission was done, then. At least I could stand up and say, "We won!" into the muzzles of the guns. Finding out she was just as damned and lost as the rest of us was a blow, I can tell you.

"I'm open to suggestions," I told her.

"Fine." She took a deep breath. "We could actually go find Jerome."

"You just said –"

"I know what I *said*. I also know that I hacked the crap out of the LMK system, and I found out where they took him."

THE NEXT MORNING, Franken was awake. Still pale, still drawn, but you wouldn't mistake him for his own corpse any more. Where he'd been shot across his chest and gut was just a load of purple bruising now, and some clenched, hard-edged scar tissue that looked months old, not hours. About his scalp, just into the hairline, I saw some livid tissue too, but right then I wrote it off, because his hair was there, and no way could they have played brain surgeon without a close shave first. I mean, that stood to reason, right?

He was sitting up, eating up our remaining rations like a starving man. When I sat by him, he managed a nod and swallowed his mouthful. His eyes headed off between the trees until they settled on some of the Finns.

"How do you feel?"

"Better," in a voice still weak, but despite that he added, "Strong." We looked at each other for a moment, and he started, "You let them...?"

I nodded, and warring expressions crossed and recrossed his face. I was waiting for him to accuse me. I wanted to say sorry, except I wasn't sorry. I expected disbelief, horror, religious mania. Instead, he took a deep breath, let it out.

The factions of his face compromised on acceptance. "Fine," he said. "Right."

Viina was already about. She moved a little gingerly but, given how she'd been shot up, the recovery was little short of miraculous. I caught her looking at me occasionally. Maybe she wanted to thank me for getting her out of it; maybe she wanted to blame me for getting her into it. No way of knowing from her face or her feline eyes.

"So, what do you reckon?" I put to Franken. "You going to be OK to move out?"

"Try me. Move out to where? We got a plan?"

"The same plan." In my mind, I turned over what Cormoran had found out. "Stockholm. Trail leads to Stockholm." Meaning that if we got there, we'd have crossed the entire breadth of Sweden from where we'd landed.

But Sturgeon had been talking to the Finns. The Finns understood everything, it seemed. Maybe they could read minds.

The Finns could help us, and I wasn't turning down anybody's hand right then, even if it had claws and hair on the palm.

CHAPTER EIGHT

THE PARTISANS WEREN'T exactly crazy about the idea, I could tell. Two days out from our unscheduled stop for rest and major surgery, and the Finns had led us south-east to another band of grim-faced locals and foisted us on them. We were clear of the US advance, which was apparently focused some way south for tactical reasons opaque to me, but the locals were digging in. This bunch were better equipped than the last – plenty more body armor, plenty better guns and plenty discipline too. Still, they knew they couldn't go toe to toe with our boys, nor with any corporate forces that might decide to give them a hard time. So I listened to them talk defiance in their civilian clothes – talk resistance and urban fighting, ambush and trap, and felt like I should do something. There was no winner, I wanted to tell them.

Nobody came out of that game well. Recent history told that story over and over.

I knew that if I said that – in the translator's confident tones that even I was starting to find unbearably smug – they'd not listen to me. I knew that plenty of them were going to die, to drones, to mechs, to us – and they'd get some of us, too. I knew. And a whole load of people who weren't fighting on anybody's side would be caught in the middle.

Don't fight, I'd tell them, and they'd stare back at me and say, *Go home*. I wished I could.

The reason this bunch were better equipped and led than most was standing in front of me right now, listening to Viina through her own tinny little Nord translator. Her name was Freya, and she was a solidly-built woman with a round, pale face and hair gathered up in a black beret, straight out of an old film about le French Resistance. She was not a partisan, exactly. She was a Nord government liaison, a political officer. She was, therefore, the enemy. I knew it, and she knew it, but apparently Viina didn't. Viina was trying to recruit her.

The interplay between the two women was very fast, and Sturgeon's commentary was erratic. Freya was angry, dismissive, incredulous, hostile. Viina was calm and focused, the sort of stillness that precedes the pounce. And she was patient; she let Freya rage and blow, and steadily wore the woman down.

"I don't get it," I told Sturgeon. "Why the hell does she think they'll do anything for us?"

"That's pretty much what this Freya wants to know, too. But Viina… I dunno, Sarge. You've seen how the Nords look at the Finns, right? Half-spooked and half in awe. Monsters, but they're *their* monsters. So now the Finns want to help us get to Stockholm without having to shoot up locals every ten miles. And this Freya can do that for us."

"So why are the *Finns* doing this for us?"

I saw where his eyes went, before he told me he didn't know. Franken was sitting a little apart, gun across his knees, brooding. He was at full strength now – you'd not even know he'd been wounded. His eyes were still blue and human, and he hadn't sprouted feathers or scales or fur. But Sturgeon and I watched him, and we waited for all these things. We waited for the alien to burst – *pop!* – out of his chest cavity. We waited to see what the Finns had done, when they saved his life. We couldn't, either of us, quite accept that saving his life was all they'd done. Every little thing, every word, every action of Franken went through a kind of filter, in our minds, where we thought, *Is that right? Is that how Franken would have done it, before?*

And of course the more we were off with him, the more he was off with us, and the more food we all served up to our paranoia.

And we didn't have any better idea of why the Finns were suddenly our best pals. It sure as well wasn't for our minimal role in saving Viina, and I didn't think that 'helping out invading US servicemen' was in their book of right things to do on principle.

"All right, fine!" said that cheerful Californian in my ear, as Freya threw up her hands. "I can get them on a train to Stockholm."

Viina followed that up with another patient demand, and a second round of negotiation began. Sturgeon translated this as centering on whether we arrived on our own two feet or handcuffed to a radiator.

"Fuck this." Franken stood abruptly, silencing the room. The Nords were big, a lot of them, but very few of them were quite as big as Franken. It was when I caught myself thinking, *Is he bigger than he used to be?* that I knew I'd gone completely nuts.

I went out – we were in a big warehouse or hangar or something, now repurposed as partisan barracks. Outside there was a carpool of random military and civilian vehicles, a couple of old sentry guns and, far too close for comfort, a little town of people who had yet to discover the joys of being bombed or driven from their homes because they were harbouring resistance fighters.

Cormoran joined me out there, hands smudged with dark oil stains from where she'd been adjusting the innards of her drone. "On a scale of one to screwed, where are we?" she asked.

I had no answers. Privately, I reckoned we'd gone off that scale some time back, but I had a care for morale, so kept the thought to myself.

WHEN WE WERE actually on the train – so too late for it to do any good – Sturgeon asked me why we hadn't just quit. We were already some way out of our skillset. We weren't black ops; we weren't special forces. We certainly shouldn't have been dolling ourselves up like Nord civilians and going on holiday to Stockholm. Yes, we had orders to bring back Cousin Jerome, but... at what point did those orders cease to bind us? It wasn't as if we hadn't pulled out before. Under fire? Low on ammo? Promised reinforcements suddenly got better things to do? Sometimes it's just better sense to fall back. But this... there was no line. There was no point at which I could say, "The mission's FUBAR, we're going home." The mission came so pre-FUBARed that I couldn't make the call.

Maybe if Cormoran had drawn a blank; maybe if there'd been no trail to follow, I'd have called it a day. But she scooped that intel out of LMK's systems, and so there we were on a train full of Nords who hadn't fancied either cosying up to the US army or taking up a gun and joining the partisans, but whose homes lay behind the lines, or would do any day. There we were, three US soldiers and a corporate stooge, and I wish I could say we were heading into the heart of darkness, but from what everyone saying about this war, it didn't even have a heart.

"How are you feeling?" I asked Franken. He'd bullied his way to a window seat, and the two of us sat awkwardly side by side in a car crammed with families. My hushed words came to him via an earpiece salvaged from his helmet, because it wouldn't do for anyone to hear a voice from the US of A right then. Oh yes, didn't I say? Only Sturgeon actually spoke the lingo, and he wouldn't pass as a local.

Our story was that we were English socialists who'd flown out here to support the cause, because apparently that was a thing. Basically we were all going to do our best Lawes impression if it came to it.

Franken shot me a narrow look. "What?" his voice growled in my ear. "Wondering if I'm feeling *Finnish?*"

"No, no." *Yes.* "It's just… You were *shot* just a couple of days ago. So I can't ask?"

"I'm fine." He stared angrily out the window at the Nord countryside speeding past. "Don't keep asking." That sounded like Franken, anyway.

So we went on to other topics, just passing the time as socialist public transport took us further and further away from the fighting. While Cormoran dozed, clutching her case, and Sturgeon read a Nord newspaper, the two of us tried to pretend that what we were doing was normal and sane. For a couple of hours we almost managed it.

I decided I'd get some shut-eye then, and hunkered down with my shoulders about my ears. The car was rowdy with people, especially screaming kids, but I had got to sleep through worse.

Only, just as I was letting myself go, Franken said something else, soft as he could, as though he didn't really want me to hear it.

"My eyes are different."

Something clenched inside me. Outwardly, I held myself calm and still, and just cocked an eye at him.

"I never saw this well before. Never." He wasn't looking at me, seemed most of the way asleep himself. I opened my mouth a couple of times, but couldn't find anything to say.

WE GOT OFF the train outside Stockholm in a flood of tired, unhappy, unwashed people. They had camps there, outside the city, and it looked like the soldiers there – gov and corp – were very keen that this tide of displaced humanity didn't wash up on their doorstep It reminded me of back home, how every so often there'd be some great cause, some refugees from one of the little wars in Asia or Africa, say, and everyone would be like, *Oh, why don't they do something?* And we'd wire a few dollars over and feel good about ourselves. Only, when New Orleans went under for good, somehow that was totally different. Franken and me, we were on crowd containment detail for that one. I got shot in Mexico the next year, and I still preferred that to the orders we got in Louisiana.

So the Nords had these camps. You know what? I've seen worse camps. They looked neat and orderly, kind of like you'd expect. For all I knew, Ikea was mass-producing a flat-pack lean-to called the 'Fükd' just for the occasion. It was still a camp, though. It was never going to be a happy place.

We weren't supposed to get off there. Political Officer Freya had given us papers to take us all the way to Stockholm Central, only we didn't trust her and so we went the last leg on foot, after Cormoran found the bugs we'd been tagged with and EMP'd them.

"Are we clean?" I asked her. No sense in making it easy for the Nords, after all.

"Clean as I can make us," she confirmed, although there was something eating at her, you could see.

"What is it?"

"When I was going over Franken," she said, eyes flicking over to find him. "It was like... I thought I'd found something for a moment – a signal of some sort. It was like something meshed with my headware, made a connection."

"But you zapped it."

"I couldn't find it. There was nothing there, nothing at all."

I felt I knew exactly what she was saying, but it was easier to play dumb. "You're not making sense."

If we'd got our teeth into the subject then, who knew how things would've played out, but instead Cormoran backed down, and I was too chicken to force the issue. "You're right," she said. "I must have been mistaken," and that was that.

Sturgeon found a delivery guy – just some package courier heading into the city on totally civilian business – and talked him into giving us a lift. This is the thing that, looking back, I find hardest to believe. Once we showed we'd got papers, though, the driver just didn't really care. We were going to give him a couple hundred dollars and he was obviously a pragmatist who reckoned a little US currency in his back pocket would be useful insurance. Cormoran sorted the money transfer and I had a sneaking suspicion she took the money from her old boss.

And so we were cut loose from Nordgov supervision and just coasted into Stockholm in the back of a van, and our papers held up when the checkpoint boys stopped us, and we thought we were terribly clever. The plan was that Cormoran would hack the local networks and send a bunch of netbots hunting for any mention of Cousin Jerome, and then they'd report back to her, and we'd bust in to wherever he was being held and GTFO just like the plan said. Or at the least we'd find out what we could and then call up Rich Ted and give him the good or bad news. That would also count as mission completed, as far as I was concerned.

So we were very clever. We were ingenious, even. For three grunts and a computer nerd we MacGyvered the fuck out of that part of the plan. We had every right to be proud of ourselves.

When we got out of the van, in a parking lot in the outskirts of Stockholm, Freya was there. She'd obviously been feeling lonely, because there were a dozen guys and girls with her who weren't in uniform, unless you count the fact that they all went to the same tailor for their suits. I guess individually they might not have drawn attention, but with that many of them together, it did kind of scream *Secret Government Agency*. They all had machine pistols, indicating that they'd already broken a few restraint barriers. I should remind you, we'd left most of our stuff behind to travel in civvies – no rifles, no helmets, just pistols and the underlayer of our body armor making us sweat under our shirts. Only now it wasn't the only thing making us sweat.

I thought the driver had sold us out, but Freya's people scared the crap out of him. He was on his knees with his hands behind his head the moment he saw them. A little star-and-stripe-painted part of me said, *That's what you get from a socialist government*, but then again it wasn't as though it didn't happen everywhere, gov or corp; so much for ideology.

We adopted the position too, and they disarmed us quite competently and took Cormoran's case.

"How'd you find us?" I asked. I felt it was expected of me.

"Not being complete idiots," said the translator in my ear, sounding as though he was enjoying it. Freya knelt down beside me, face to face, her gun pressed to my side.

"I don't think you're a bad man, Sergeant Regan." Now she was speaking English, crisp and unaccented. "But I don't know why you're here in my city – maybe you don't even know yourself. I don't trust anything that comes out of the US lines right now. So I can't just give you the run of Stockholm, no matter what the Finns say. Because I don't trust them, either."

"So what now?" I was wondering if I could grab her, hold her hostage. Problem was that the Nords had more hostages than I could realistically hold on to, and there was nothing to stop them putting a bullet in the back of Sturgeon's head to show me how serious they were.

"You come back to our place and we ask you some questions. Politely, the first time. But I think you know the drill."

One of them took the van man off. Another shoved us in the back of an armored car painted up in the blue and neon yellow of the local law and order. We were cuffed to the interior, with a couple guys to watch over us and another couple in the cab. The rest of the Men In Black got into other vehicles with prominent government plates. Apparently inner Stockholm is a no-car zone unless you're gov or corp or very rich, which I guess really hampers your ability to cruise about in unmarked cars being sinister and anonymous.

There wasn't much conversation in the back of the prison wagon, mostly because our guards shouted at anyone who spoke. Sturgeon looked philosophical and Cormoran was fretting about her case, I thought.

Franken looked... not good. His jaw was clenched and one of his eyes was half-closed. He looked like a man with toothache. When I caught his gaze, he winced and looked away. There was sweat on his forehead, as though he was running a fever.

I was about to make something of it – everyone's seen the movie where the prisoner's sick, so the guards suddenly abandon all pretense at security. But then we stopped – and quite suddenly – and things obviously went south outside because there was shooting.

Our captors didn't know what to do. They tried for orders, but got nothing from their radios. We saw through the grill that the two guys in the cab got out – and then one of them fell right back in, only deader than when he'd left. There was a quick meeting of minds in the back of the car, which we were not invited to attend, and then our two guys kicked the back door open and went out guns first.

They put them away sharpish, because there were a bunch of guys outside in full urban ops gear with assault rifles, waiting for them. It was the slickest work I ever saw, how they bundled the gov types away and then cut us loose and got us out. We were in the middle of the city, some old part where all the buildings looked like someone had repurposed Disneyland for offices – I saw skewed vans ahead where they'd blocked off the leading gov cars. I heard sirens, but they were going to be too late. Freya's remaining people were keeping their heads well down.

So the lot of us got bundled into more cars with gov plates – either they were stolen or faked, or there were just more govs in Nordland that I'd been led to believe. I saw Freya and some of her survivors sent off that way, and then it was our turn. Nobody was explaining what was going on, and none of the super-stealthy black ops uniforms had handy badges to tell us who these new guys were. Except better equipped and more ruthless than our original captors, which suggested to me they must be corp types of some description.

They frisked us over for bugs. They even zapped something in Cormoran's headware because they thought it would let her call out. It obviously hurt like hell when they did it – moving some sort of gadget up to her temples and letting fly. One of her eyes was bloodshot, after that, and I had the horrible thought that they'd fried some of her actual brain rather than just the tech. When she'd got over the shock of it, though, she found a moment to meet my gaze and wink that red eye. Apparently she had a trick up her cybernetic sleeve even then.

We ended up somewhere in central Stockholm, that's all I knew. We got head-bagged after a while, and we were moved between vehicles and made to bumble along on foot. We went underground for a bit, from the echoes, and we went in lifts and on moving floorways. If we'd come out of it in some secret volcano lair, I wouldn't have been much surprised.

And then the bags came off, and the cuffs came off, and we were all four of us in a board room overlooking the commercial district from somewhere high up.

CHAPTER NINE

Stockholm's one of those Euro cities where most of it looks like – well, like Euro cities are supposed to, if you're from the States – all old, old stuff as though any moment a bunch of people in wigs and enormous dresses are going to pour out and start doing one of those old-timey dances.

There's a few bits in the middle, though, where the last century's caught up to it. There's one part that Sturgeon tells me is called something like 'The Wall of Glass' now – they had one big skyscraper there, and then another and another, all crammed in because other parts of the city were just too damn historical to knock down, until it was like Superman's Fortress of Solitude around there, just a great big bank of glass and steel. And all solar-collectors, of course, because this is the Nords we're talking about.

Anyway, that's where we were, and the serious-looking men who'd put us there were leaving, ceding the room to us. We had a whole-wall window onto that part of the city, all bright and lit up and advertising weird-ass Nord products on its big eyesore video billboards. Another wall was all screens, as though someone was going to ask us to make a presentation any minute.

"Everyone OK?" I asked first. Sturgeon nodded, but Cormoran was frowning. She indicated her head and then a wave of her fingers at the room around us. No connectivity, apparently.

"Franken," I pressed, because he hadn't answered.

"Fine," he grunted. He didn't look fine. His hands were fists, and I could see the muscles of his neck twitch and tic. Cued by me, the other two stared at him as well and he rounded on us angrily. "I'm fine, OK? Get off my back, for Chrissake!"

Sturgeon was going to say something at the uncharacteristic cussing, but Franken loomed at him and snapped, "*I'm allowed, all right?*"

I put a hand on his shoulder, and although he shrugged it off angrily, he stood still while I said, quiet as I could, "Tell me."

There was real fear in his eyes, deep down where only I could see. "I can hear... it's like there's voices, right at the edge of everything. It's like there's a radio inside my head, with the volume turned real low."

Then Sturgeon said, "Someone's coming," but he didn't need to. We all knew it because, despite the reinforced floors that corp towers had these days, you could still feel it through your feet when a Scion was on the way. And no wonder they'd left us alone with our thoughts, because it wasn't as though we could do much against one of them.

The seven foot chrome exoskeleton that walked in was stepping lightly, for what it was. It paused in the door, regarding the four of us. Its barrel torso was broad enough around that I guessed the rich kid was sitting down in there, and the limbs were pure mech – it could go either way, with those shells. The head atop it was bland and faceless: purely decorative, or maybe full of guns.

I came halfway to standing to attention, all three of us army types did. It was what you did with Scions, when they weren't actively trying to kill you.

"Sergeant First Class Theodore Patrick Regan," a pleasant male voice named me, well spoken and American. "Specialist Soloman Sturgeon; Specialist Daniel Belweather Franken, all of the United States 203rd Infantry Division." There was a snicker from Sturgeon because that was the first any of us had heard of Franken's middle name, which sure as hell wasn't on any of his ID. That there was no answering snarl worried me more than I could say.

"And Miss Helena Cormoran," the Scion went on, "formerly with the Special Corporate Services Division of Huesson International Technology and Logistics Incorporated." The faceless metal head made a show of scanning the room. "What happened to the other one?"

"Lead poisoning," I answered.

The Scion made an amused sound, nodding philosophically

as if the head was real. It took up a position at the head of the board table, as though about to chair a meeting or call up a pie chart on the screens behind it. "I understand you've come a long way to find me."

I gave that gleaming face a long, hard stare. "Nice try."

But then it was splitting open, just peeling back, and the chest and shoulders as well, the metal hinging, folding and flexing, until the body was half-open. It wasn't something any of us had seen before; the whole point of being a Scion was that you were in your own little impregnable world. You didn't open up where us lowlifes might throw a punch. But this one did. In that office tower on the far side of Nordland, we got to see how the other half live when they go to war.

Or at least the head and shoulders of it, anyway, it didn't unzip all the way and spill him out. It was cosy in there, I can confirm, and he was cushioned by all sorts of direct interface gear – to give him instant living control of the shell, and to keep his body fit and suppress its complaining for as long as he needed to stay inside. Tell the truth, I wasn't really looking. I was looking at his face instead. Within the steel was Cousin Jerome, in the flesh, with a grin that was pure rich boy mischief.

"That's right, Sergeant."

"But your shell," I got out. "We saw it, with…"

"Yes, you did crash our friends from LMK, didn't you? Who aren't exactly happy about that, by the way. I had to leave my shell there, Sergeant. They're just too easy to track. But we made sure I had a pristine new suit of clothes waiting at this end, as part of the deal." And then it all went in reverse, and we were face to face with that shiny façade again, except now his face got projected onto it, like Rich Ted's had been. There was more than one way to show a family resemblance.

"What deal?" Franken said, sounding strained. When I glanced at him, he looked in pain, one hand pressed to his jaw. His other twitched out and touched the shell of the Scion. I'd seen it done, before a battle: the superstitious seeking some metal benediction, as if having had all that money's worth of titanium and steel under your hand would rub off, somehow. I wondered if he was praying, if he wanted the sheer concentrated wealth to drive the Finnish right out of him like an exorcism.

Jerome Speling's visage frowned and flickered. "Is your man ill?" His light-built features adopted an expression of concern.

"He got shot," I said shortly. "And what deal? We were told to rescue you. We were told the Nords got you, that they had some sort of super-weapon that switched off your suit. But you're saying that you…"

"Switched it off myself? I did, yes." The hand he lifted could have crushed iron girders. "Don't look at me like that. I'm no traitor. I came here to arrange the end of the war."

"The end…?" And suddenly it made sense. Of course he did. His corporation – that big multinational where the board and shareholders all had his nose and his chin – wouldn't want a drawn-out expensive war after all, even if the US gov was footing most of the bill. And the Nords must have seen already that their tech wasn't as good as ours. Of course we'd send someone, quiet and covert, to negotiate their surrender. It all fell into place.

Except for the pieces that just kept falling, like *us*. I was working my way to saying it when Cormoran broke in.

"When the US government wants to talk terms, they send a diplomat," she pointed out quietly. "And they don't need to go all hush hush because that's what diplomats do: they go to other countries and talk at our enemies. I'm guess you weren't sent by the White House, Mr Speling."

"There are those with considerably more at stake here than the government, after all," he agreed equably. "Come on, now, I'm sure none of you are quite that naïve."

"Wars start and stop for corporate interest," Sturgeon agreed darkly, and I shot him a warning look. This really wasn't the place for his polemic.

There was a weird thing then, because the screens behind the Scion flickered, and one of them began to play a movie, only it was a movie of Cousin Jerome talking to some other guys. Open Scion shells were behind the others, like they'd all decided to show how much they trusted each other by stepping out. What was behind Jerome was the camera, so we were mostly seeing the back of his head unless he looked left or right.

I assumed the point of this would become relevant later, so I didn't say anything about it. None of us did.

"Well, quite." It really was quite amazing how natural and human the body language of that man-shaped vehicle was, with its idle gestures, waving away Sturgeon's words. "The old nationalist way of waging war was ruinous, after all. Easier just to know from the start that it's about protecting business interests. What is our great country, after all, without its industry? And so, when it's about money from the start, then it ends when both sides know they're not going to get any richer by letting it carry on."

"Linköping," said Franken. It sounded like he was trying to clear something from his throat. The weirdest thing was that the image of Jerome on the screen kind of lip-synced with the word.

Jerome – the real Jerome – might or might not have heard him, but Cormoran grabbed at his attention as soon as he'd finished speaking.

"That still doesn't make sense," she objected. "Did your cousin not know about this deal? Because if he did, it must have slipped his mind when he was giving us our orders. We're supposed to be getting you back behind the lines..." but her voice tailed off as she said it, and she glanced at me helplessly. "Or..."

Jerome let the pause become awkward before speaking to fill it. "Unfortunately, a high-ranking Scion such as myself can't just step off the radar, Miss Cormoran."

"Ms," she corrected flatly. "So, while I can't say I had any illusions, how about you explain to the Sergeant exactly what that means, Mr Speling."

I didn't need the explanation. "We weren't supposed to succeed," I said hollowly. "The world was meant to think you'd been got. Which meant the world would expect someone to be sent after you. Which meant us, because we were supposed to have fuck all chance of actually getting this far. And, Cormoran, I'm sorry, because you've pretty much been telling me this from the start."

"Pretty much," she agreed.

"Jönåker," said Franken, more clearly this time, and it was weird, because he didn't speak a word of Nord, but he was saying it with just those sort of weird stresses and sounds the locals gave words.

And this time Jerome had heard him. The metal suit went very still and he demanded, "What did he say?"

"Hanukah, I think." Sturgeon looked only baffled.

But Cousin Jerome suddenly had a bee in his metal bonnet, and he came stomping around to tower over Franken. "You say that again!"

Franken lifted his head, and his face was agony, pale and sweat-sheened. "They say Linköping. They say Jönåker. The battles you planned." Suddenly he leapt back with his hands to his head. "Get out!" he screamed. "I don't want to know. I don't want to tell them! Linköping! Jönåker! Bergshammar!"

"What the hell?" was my contribution.

"Places, Nord places." Cormoran must have had some maps stored in her headware. "Drawing a line from our advance to Stockholm." And half the rest of the screens all lit up showing Jeromev – different meetings, different people: rich men sitting together to plan the fate of the rest of the world. Some of it was from building security cams, but most wasn't footage that anyone would have wanted recorded for posterity. But Jerome's new shell had been kept running, in case things went south and he needed to bail into it. It had recorded everything its master had done.

Then Jerome lunged forward and caught up Franken, one hand clenching on the man's arm, one at his throat, hoisting him bodily. The questions erupting out of his shell were the only things keeping Franken alive. The projected face had frozen in mid-smile, like the man inside had died.

"Tell me how you know that!" he demanded. "You can't know that. You were checked; you've got nothing that can cut into our data. You couldn't change the channels on a TV with the 'ware we left you."

"Fuck!" Cormoran leapt up from where she'd been sitting. "Oh you son of a bitch!" Whatever she was looking at was not in the room.

I remembered when she said she thought something in Franken had touched her headware. I remembered it wasn't there when she'd gone back for it. I wondered what the hell sort of shapeshifting bioware the Finns had put in Franken's skull just so he could get inside this building and let them reach out and touch the enemy's network.

There were maps springing up on the rest of the screens – troop movements, figures, documents in English and Swedish. Cormoran had put as much of the room as possible between her and Jerome, not that it would have helped.

"I'm getting their plan fed directly into my implants," she got out, shaking her head frantically. "I've no idea how. Nord forces meet US advance at Linköping, get their asses kicked. Try to hold at Jönåker, get their asses kicked. Then…" her eyes, white and red, were very wide. "Oh hell."

"Not another word!" Jerome warned her, advancing around the table with Franken still held aloft.

"Sergeant, they're going to bring down the government, the Swedish government. It's all set out, clear as day. They'll manufacture unrest after Jönåker, topple the socialists, get a corp puppet regime in place that'll do exactly what they want." She was gabbling it out, scuttling crabwise about the table to keep it between them.

Jerome put a stop to that by throwing Franken into the table, which snapped it in half and should have done the same to him.

"And what's wrong with that?" the Scion demanded. "That's what we want, isn't it? A compliant Nordgov that will do what we ask, what the Nord corps ask, whatever's best for business? Why are you saying this as though it's a bad thing?"

"Wait, so what was the other one?" I asked, into the silence that followed. "Link-thing and Hanukah and…"

"Bergshammar," Cormoran pronounced. "Bergshammar is where the Nords throw us back, in this plan. To give confidence to their new government they need a victory over our guys." It was like she was reading it from an autocue inside her head. "After that, everyone sits down at the peace table and everyone gets what they want. Except for the Nord people I guess. And except for everyone who got stage-managed to death in the fighting."

"All right, fine," Jerome said, sounding very calm again. "So let's change the topic of conversation onto *how the fuck you just did that*?" And the crazy was right back, the crazy of a man who's had things his own way since he was born, and suddenly doesn't. "There are no signals. Our techs have checked. Nothing's getting out of this room."

Sturgeon cleared his throat nervously. "You might want to get them to check again." He was standing at the window, looking out at Stockholm's swanky business district. All the billboards, all those great big electric adverts, they were showing Jerome. They were showing Jerome's maps. They were showing, piecemeal but coherent, Jerome's plan.

Jerome took two steps toward the glass wall. The attitude of the suit was shorn of all humanity, as if it had just been an act he was putting on.

"They made me do it." The voice, sepulchral, came from the wreckage of the table. Franken sat up, cut and bloody, but still in one piece. "They used me. They're in my head. They needed me to get here so they could hack your system from inside. They work best when they're close to things."

"Our system is locked down," the Scion spat out, "Nothing is getting out. The moment you got brought in we made *sure*. Just in... just in case... We killed *her* connections. We made certain. You were scanned and... scanned..." By then, his voice was almost a whimper.

"I can hear them," Franken lurched to his feet. "They're in my head, all the time. I'm in theirs. They work best when they're close to things. But them and me – even when we're far away, we're still close to each other. We're all together.

We're all equal in the pack." And then a sudden burst of the old Franken as he turned to me and cried out, "Fuck's sake, Sarge, they made me into a commie!"

I don't know whether it was that aggrieved capitalist soul of his or some instinct of the Finnish network that he was plugged into, but he just went for Jerome then. He rammed into him with his full bodyweight, and although the Scion must have weighed half a ton, Franken hit him high up and toppled him toward the windows.

And life's not the movies, and they build tower blocks pretty damn strong. Jerome hammered into the glass and cracked it a thousand ways, but it didn't give. He ended up hanging there, actually half out over the street and stuck in the crazed glass like it was a spiderweb.

I knew my cue. "Go!" I yelled.

A couple of the corp security who'd grabbed us were already in the doorway, weapons up. Franken just about used Jerome's chest as a footplate to spring at them. I saw two holes punched in him – all the way through – and then he had slammed the corp guys down to the ground. He was weeping. He threw them around like they were dolls but he was weeping. His face was knotted up like a fist with self-loathing. Blood streamed from his wounds but it was already thick and clotting. They were flesh wounds, literally: punched through muscle that was already knitting itself together.

I got one gun and Franken got the other and the four of us burst out into the next room, and then the room after, because a lot of people were getting the hell out of Dodge around then. It wasn't even Franken lighting a fire under their asses – right then the whole building seemed to be in utter chaos.

CHAPTER TEN

MOVIES AGAIN: YOU know, the ones where the hero's fighting the bad guys in a tower block. You saw that one where they're fighting all the way down the stairwell, or there's that one they remade like nine times, where the guy drops bombs down the elevator shaft and they magically know to explode just where the villain's guys are. Did you once see one of those where the hero got lost? Seriously, if we hadn't actually seen the fire escape sign we'd be wandering round there still. Nobody stopped to engage us in a complicated martial arts fight. In fact, most of the guys we saw around there didn't look as though fighting people was why they were on the payroll. They were in suits or shirtsleeves. Some of them were just running around, but a lot of them were at computers very determinedly doing something –

Cormoran said they were wiping data, reformatting drives. Others were actually shredding paper documents, like they were having a flashback to two decades before. We saw a lot of LMK letterheads and logos, and I reckoned their stock was probably underperforming on the exchange right about then, because if that crap was on the billboards outside, then it would be all the way around the world by now. There'd be guys in China selling their shares in LMK even as we were trying to get out of the building.

So we found some stairs, and for a moment we stopped there, breathing heavily and listening to the sound of running feet and panicked voices. It wasn't just the stock market crash these people were worried about. While me and mine were focused on trivialities like just how many good men would die to bring about Jerome's little plan, I reckoned the Socialist Government of Sweden would be more interested in that whole corporate-assisted regime change thing.

"Franken," Sturgeon said. "Franken. *Bellweather*, you all right?"

Franken was crouched down on the steps, holding his head like he was trying to tear it off. "Don't call me that," he grated.

"Then give us a sign, man," Sturgeon insisted. "Come on, what's up with you?"

"They're telling me... they're telling me to do things," he rasped out.

"Tell them to fuck off," was my advice.

"I can hear them. They say up, we go up... up, up, up."

"Can they hear me?" I demanded, and in the absence of a cogent reply I went on, "You listen here, you Finnish bastards. You've got what you wanted. You've got your spy into this place and ripped open its guts. You can leave him alone now. We don't need you any more."

Franken's head swivelled to look at me, eyes very wide, the pupils like pinpricks. What was wrenched out of his lips wasn't English. To me it didn't sound human, but Sturgeon had his inner Finnish-human dictionary working overtime and he said, "It – he – Franken says we need to get to the roof. He says to trust... them."

Not a chance, but Cormoran was already filling in from intel they were feeding her. "Sarge, they've got army and police pulling up all around this place. What are they going to think when a bunch of Americans try to push past them."

"That we're part of the problem," I finished for her. "Fine. Okay. But what's up?"

"Helipad," Cormoran said flatly.

"We're short a helicopter."

"I reckon they'll be flying one in for the big cheeses."

I grimaced. "Fine but – Sturgeon, ask Franken – ask whoever's in there with him if we get him *back* at the end of this. Ask them if they can make him right."

"Sarge, I don't even think they'd understand the question," Sturgeon said.

Then Franken stood, and that was plainly our cue. We were up those stairs at a solid soldier's pace, glad for once we'd had to leave our packs behind.

Nobody in the world knew who we were or what part

we'd played right then. But everyone knew what had been done. As we were thundering up those stairs – occasionally elbowing aside locals who were far more sensibly heading *down* – the material the Finns had hacked out of Jerome's shell and the LMK net was on a thousand websites, broadcast in a hundred countries. Sure, it was pored over by countless emergency gov and corp committees, but that wasn't the thing, because those people knew the score already. The big deal was that now everyone *else* got to see how the deals were done. Everyone else, who'd been told about national interest and liberty and freedom and ideals, was being given a chance to wake up and smell that stuff they'd always told us was roses.

And you know what? I know what Sturgeon has to say about the whole deal, but Sturgeon says a lot of things. Me? I don't get that having the gov types run the show is so great, or the corps either. But when someone has me bent over the table and tells me to smile when I get shafted; when someone has their eye on their shareholder dividend so much that they're willing to get my people killed for it; that's going to get even me into politics.

Up the stairs, and I had to catch Cormoran as she stumbled. She had a hand pressed to her face, and my stomach lurched with, *Jesus, it's catching?* as if being Finnish was contagious now. But she shook her head quickly. "Gonna have to cover for me, Sergeant," she said. "I'm... rebooting my headware. Got all kinds of shit streaming past my eyes right now. I'm trying to get a comms channel out past the burnt sectors. Not going to be much good until I'm done."

I held onto her as we slogged up and up, all the time not knowing what we'd find at the top.

And then we were up, and we were late to the party because the Board of LMK had already turned up for the evac party. There were three of them in the building at that time, or at least that was all who'd made it the roof. Probably I'd have recognized faces from the Jerome tapes currently breaking box office records all over the world, but of course their faces and the rest of them were hidden behind their metal shells. These were all Family men, scions of whatever the Swedish corporate dynasties were.

Crouched at the top of the stairwell I demanded, "So what's the plan now?" in a hoarse whisper. "Firstly, I don't see them making room on the chopper for us; secondly, how the hell is LMK even going to fly one in without the Nord flyboys taking it down? I'm willing to bet that they really, *really* want these guys to answer some questions."

"No idea about the first," said Sturgeon, "but for the second: incoming."

The air, which had been hosting sirens and the occasional gunshot from far, far below, began to thrum with a familiar thunder. It wasn't the sound of a nice corporate helicopter with all mod cons, not even the heavy lifters the Scions used. It was something bigger. 'Bigger' didn't do it justice, in fact. The only word was *Biggest*.

A vast shadow was falling over Stockholm as the largest, ugliest combat flier in the world taxied awkwardly over the city center toward LMK's doomed corporate HQ. The White Russians were bringing their Jodorowsky, still scarred from its run in with the 203rd but no less dangerous for all of that.

One of the Scions stepped forward, waving. Another took that moment to glance back, and obviously spotted us. It turned smartly and began striding toward us.

"Back down the stairs!" I ordered, and Franken promptly bolted out across the roof like a startled rabbit.

I thought he was charging the Scion, but he was cutting a path around it, close to the rooftop's railing, as if making a desperate break for the helipad. Of course we went after him, but the Scion was already between us, gaining on him despite his burst of speed.

The other two were turning, alerted by their fellow VIP. Beyond them, the Jodorowsky drew closer. I saw something strike fire off it, some Nordgov gunship or ground to air, and it replied with a contemptuous salvo, not even altering its course.

The running Scion had almost caught up with Franken when it tripped. It cracked the concrete when it came down, then lurched up to its knees. At first I couldn't see what was going on, but there were grey shadows clinging to it, three at least, and there were more coming over the edge of the roof. They climbed like spiders, four hundred feet of glass and steel. They must have been scaling the building since we were brought in. The Finns, of course. They hadn't been as far away as the voice in Franken's head had made him think.

I saw one grasped by those metal hands and ripped in two. Even the best bioscience can't toughen you up to resist the full torsion strength of a well-made Scion. The others were already at work, though. They weren't trying to get through that immaculate shell; they simply didn't have the strength. They had an ally, though – a big one: gravity.

Scions weighed most of a ton, but they were made to be as light as possible whilst remaining impregnably strong. Three Finn werewolves could hoist one in the air easily enough, and then it was over the railing with him, because even if the outer armor didn't crack open, the occupant would be so much jello when it hit the street.

Automatic fire sprayed from another Scion – I saw at least a couple of the Finns go down, injured and writhing. The rest were already on their targets then, driving them away from the helipad and toward the roof's edge.

They lost more than a few, the Finns, but they fought like... I want to say animals, but that gives the wrong impression. They fought like a pack, perfectly coordinated, each one selfless and totally committed to the cause. They had those metal men off the side of the building faster than you'd believe. All the while we just stood there, Sturgeon and I, and Cormoran crouched at our feet trying to get her head together, muttering to herself.

The Finns vanished over the edge of the roof as quickly as they'd come, job done, skittering down the building's sides like nightmares. Then it was just us and the Jodorowsky, which had come in to hover impossibly above us, like a meteorite impact about to happen. And then, even as it lurched and shifted for balance in the air, it was us, the Jodorowsky and Jerome Spelman in his metal suit.

He was pissed. I think I can say that for certain. He burst out onto the roof still spiky with glass from the window. He had geared up, too. There were a couple of weapon pods over his shoulders ready to unleash hell in our general direction.

This was the moment for noble speeches, but I had nothing. There are reasons I never made it past Sergeant.

We retreated as far as we could go, but no matter how big the tower, there was still only so much distance we could get on the roof. Jerome took three steps and braced but, because of who he was, because we had really got him riled over and above anyone in his whole life, he let us have the benefit of his opinion first.

"You've got them thinking I'm a traitor," came his amplified voice. "You piece of fucking white trailer trash! I was going to end the war! *I'm* the patriot here! You're the traitors! And now I'm going to put you in your fucking place with a fucking vengeance."

And the rooftop shuddered and flared with artillery, the whole structure of the building shaking and cracking with the fury of it. I didn't see much of the result, because I was instantly half-deaf and half-blind, crouching like a sinner at the second coming. The Jodorowsky had opened up on Jerome.

"– the hell?" Sturgeon was shouting, wide-eyed as a kid at a fireworks display. "... do that for?"

"I asked him to!" Cormoran hollered over the thunderous echoes bouncing back and forth between my ears. "I got a channel out! I called the pilot!"

"Why's he on our side now?" I demanded.

"I promised him my old boss's bank access codes!"

"Sarge –!"

Sturgeon's shout dragged my focus round to the slag and rubble that had been the other half of the roof. We could see a fair amount of the building's twisted skeleton through it, and sure as hell nobody was coming up those stairs again, nor were we leaving that way. What we could also see was Jerome.

He was crouched on all fours, and one of his weapon pods was mangled. His shiny shell was all battered to crap, but he was very much still with us. Even as I saw him, he began launching at the Jodorowsky, and although his shots looked tiny compared to the gunship's, the vast frame above us rocked and groaned when they struck. The best that money can buy, like I said. I figure that each shot Jerome took was worth a year's back pay for the whole 203rd.

Cormoran was shouting – in Russian no less – at the pilot, who was presumably trying very hard not to drop down and squish the lot of us.

Franken was already at Jerome.

I hadn't seen him go. I still don't know what drove him, whether he was a puppet of the Finns in that moment, or a loyal friend and comrade, or just so tortured by what they'd done to him that he would take any way out.

Jerome was already on shaky footing on the tangled wreckage of the roof, and the recoil from his own ordnance didn't help. Then Franken slammed into him at top speed, grappling him by the head and the ruined weapons pod.

For a moment I didn't think it had helped, but then Jerome was tilting stiffly backward, like a dictator's statue hauled down by an angry mob. I saw his arms reach for balance as he took one teetering step back and then another, but there was nothing there for that second step, and he dropped, falling away past the mangled girders and shattered concrete and the million shards of glass.

And then the Jodorowsky unrolled a metal ladder at us with a clatter, and it was time for us to make our getaway. The three of us. Just the three of us.

THERE WAS A very awkward meeting, two days after that. Present were: me, Sturgeon and Cormoran, Political Officer Freya, Viina the Finn and a Russian named Genaddy Osipov. Our lack of tech finally became a positive because they had to conduct the whole business in English, and I listened to Freya's translator speak clipped sentences into her ear with all the verve of a tax accountant, while Genaddy's murmured in a breathy female voice that seemed to be constantly on the point of orgasm.

Of the lot of us, only Genaddy was happy. A common soldier in the White Russians' mercenary companies, he had suddenly become richer to the tune of several million dollars thanks to Cormoran's hurried negotiation. He grinned at everyone and drank from a hip flask, and it wasn't entirely clear why he was there except that he was hard to shake off.

The subject of our discussion was mostly extradition. Nordgov would happily have vanished us away to an interrogation camp somewhere, I knew, but it had become fairly well known that we'd thwarted a corporate coup, however unwittingly, so we were somehow heroes of the exact nation we had come over to make war on. The one upside was that we weren't easily vanishable.

There were a lot of calls for us to go back home, some of which wanted to put us on trial, while others wanted to pin medals on us. I'd found a TV giving CNN with Swedish subtitles, and discovered that things were busy back Stateside. The revelations about how the war was being fought – about who was pulling the strings – had led to enough popular uproar that suddenly Congress and Senate were both trying to look shocked. There would be enquiries, and people were already talking about wars past: Canada, Mexico, Somalia, the intervention in Chile. Suddenly a lot of recent military history was looking fishy. The Swedish campaign was already being rolled back, our boys heading home early and in one piece. The TV was full of politicians trying to out-do each other in crusading against the very scourge of the American people that had probably put them in office. There was talk of a New New Deal, of expanded regulation, anti-trust stuff. Who knew whether it would come to anything? Meanwhile the markets were in free fall. I thought about all those expensive Scion suits and wondered how much would have to get struck from the portfolios of the wealthy before they couldn't afford them anymore.

In the end, Sturgeon accepted political asylum in Sweden. He always was a socialist at heart, and he had no faith in the reception we might receive back home. Cormoran negotiated a service tour with the Russians, because their money was good, and she likewise didn't fancy her chances in a country that had become an unwelcoming place for an educated black woman over the last few decades.

For me, I could see only one choice. The US was where I came from, and it was where I was going to. I wanted to see this through. I wanted to rejoin the 203rd. I wanted to testify to what little I knew. Most of all, I didn't want to turn my back on what Franken had believed in. I said so, to the lot of them. I said it to Sturgeon's face, after he'd done moralizing. I said it to Freya. I said it to Viina: that I would honor his memory; that Franken had always been a good American boy.

And she looked at me then, with an expression on her face – but with those Finns it was hard to read anything they let show. I tried to ask questions, through Sturgeon, but she just pretended she couldn't understand him. And yet her eyes never left me, and that look never left her. *I know something you don't.*

I chewed over that look all the way until I was waiting for the diplomatic helicopter to come repatriate me. I got to wondering just what might have happened to Jerome and to Franken when they fell. There was a lot of broken building they might have bounced off on the way. Could Franken have lived? Was that what Viina's ambiguous expression had been trying to tell me?

But by then I was already in the air, and whatever secrets Viina had, she'd taken them back to the dark, science-haunted no-fly zone that was Finland.